FELIX

Boyfriend For Hire, Book 5

_____

RJ SCOTT
MEREDITH RUSSELL

Love Lane Books

Felix, Boyfriend for Hire, Book 5

Copyright © 2022 by RJ Scott

Copyright © 2022 by Meredith Russell

Cover design by Meredith Russell

Edited by Sue Laybourn

ISBN: 9781785645433

Published by Love Lane Books Ltd

RJ ~ Always for my family.

Meredith ~ For my family and friends for their continued love and support.

Felix

Hiring a fake boyfriend for a school reunion seems to be the only solution, but love was never part of the equation.

Felix has enough on his plate looking out for his parents, let alone agreeing to be hired for a date with the friend of a friend. His instant attraction to the scatter-brained scientist has him making impulsive decisions he hopes he won't regret. But, somehow, he's agreeing to more dates, and more time with sexy Ethan and his non-stop talking. When stolen wintry kisses turn to love, and Christmas works its magic, Felix knows he's losing his heart.

The science of chemistry makes more sense to Ethan than connecting with potential boyfriends, and he's wary of romance. Unsettled by a string of failed hookups, he knows it's on him when everything goes wrong, and he can't help but wonder what has made him this way. His friend Jared says that Ethan needs to close metaphorical doors on past hurts—whatever that means—and that the school reunion might just be step one. Determined to show himself as confident and happy, he hires Felix to be his date for the night, but after a kiss to make up for the one he missed at prom, abruptly, it's not the past that is consuming his thoughts.

Now all Felix has to do is show Ethan that it's okay to love, and be loved in return, and that chemistry can lead to a happily ever after.

Boyfriend for Hire

FELIX

RJ SCOTT & MEREDITH RUSSELL

Love Lane Books

Chapter One

"I'm leaving the office now." Felix stopped at the top of the steps to the building housing the Bryant & Waites offices. "I should be with you within the hour."

He looked up, shielding his eyes with his free hand as soft snowflakes fluttered about him. The winter sun was low, hazy through a thin layer of wispy white cloud in the pinkish, early evening sky. With a sigh, he balanced his cellphone between his ear and shoulder, and struggled with the zipper of his jacket. The office had been warm, and he had forgotten just how cold the weather waiting for him outside was. He let out a hum when he pulled up the zipper and buried his chin in the collar of his jacket.

"Did Gideon say anything about what happened last month?" Jared asked on the other end of the call.

Felix sighed. Last month had been hell—he'd been booked for a high-profile client, but his dad had fallen ill, and he'd had to back out at the last minute. Jared had stepped in, and Felix was grateful for that help and the fact he still had a job.

"Nothing awful; he was fine." Felix gripped his phone and raised his head. "Or seemed to be. Gave me his *I understand* face. You know where he does that pout thing and nods a lot?"

Jared laughed. "Ah. I usually get a lot of sighing when I'm called into his office."

"That's because you mess up way too often. Or you did before Nate. You've been with Nate about a year now, right?"

"Nearly a year and a half."

"Took long enough, but I guess he's—finally—having a good influence on you."

"Maybe he is." Felix could hear the smile in Jared's voice.

"Maybe." Felix echoed. "Anyway, you did me a favor covering that contract at the last minute, so once again, I say *thank you*."

"Don't worry about it. How's your dad?"

Felix huffed a breath and took the steps down to the sidewalk, taking care not to fall over.

A few days before the four-day contract, Felix's dad had missed his footing and taken a tumble down some steps. The fall had left him bruised and with a broken arm, and Felix had been glad it hadn't been worse. Needing to take care of both his dad and his mom, who'd had a stroke a few years back and was in a wheelchair, while his dad was laid up, Felix had been desperate to withdraw from the contract. When even

Caleb-I'll-take-any-job-Harris couldn't help, Jared had stepped in.

"Fine. Well, he's irritable and tells me several times a day how he wants the cast off. He's driving both me and Mom crazy. It'll be a few more weeks before he can be free of it." He checked either way before taking the last step and fell in behind a couple with a stroller. "Gideon suggested that I just do single-day dates for the foreseeable future. I agreed."

Felix preferred the short contracts anyway—dates to functions or parties lasting an afternoon, an evening, a few hours. He found the jobs where he had to act at being in love for long periods of time tiring, and, in some ways, he disliked the insincerity and the feelings of guilt that sometimes lingered after spending days in the company of a client's family and friends, getting to know them. But it was a job, one that, nine times out of ten, he enjoyed. The money was good, and it gave him a chance to experience people and places he'd never have been able to otherwise.

"That's great," Jared said. "Anyway, we can talk more when you get here."

"You're seriously not going to tell me what's this *favor* you want?"

"Nope. I'll tell you when I see you."

With a sigh, Felix pushed his free hand into his jacket. "Fine. I'm heading to you now."

"Later."

Felix hung up, then quickened his pace, spotting room to slip past the small family, and jogged a few steps along the wet sidewalk to get in front of them. He glanced over his shoulder, smiling as he laid eyes on the toddler. The young boy was grinning from beneath the hood of the stroller and held a large superhero doll in his gloved hands.

Cute kid.

He'd often wanted a younger sibling when he was growing up. He was an only child, his parents not having had him until they were in their forties. A lot of his parents' friends had older children in their families, so he was usually the youngest. He figured Jared had come the closest to filling the role of a younger brother. The two of them had gotten close after being paired up for a joint hire nine months ago. A pair of siblings had wanted partners while attending a fashion show event and its afterparty. A broken six-inch heel and a spilled glass of red, and it had fallen to Felix to quash Jared's good intentions and get the date back on track.

He made his way to the station and onto the platform and took the chance to text his dad and let him know his meeting was over, and he was on his way to Jared's. When all he got was an *okay* in reply, he followed up with a reminder that dinner was already made and just needed reheating.

There was an announcement over the speakers as the train pulled into the station. Pocketing his phone, he boarded, standing near the doors for the few stops, until they reached the station nearest Jared's neighborhood. At least, it was Jared's for now. He was already as good as moved in with his boyfriend, Nate, and using the old apartment he shared with a guy called Ethan as a glorified storage unit.

After a brief, brisk walk in the snow, he was at the door.

"Hey," Jared said. "Come in." He stepped back, opening the door wide.

"Thanks." Warmth and the rich, meaty smell of food hit him as he entered the apartment. He slipped off his jacket, shrugging it from his shoulders as he made his way through to the living room. He stopped, raising an eyebrow as he faced Jared's roommate who stiffened on seeing him, sitting bolt upright on the sofa. He'd only been to the apartment a couple of times before and had, until then, never crossed paths with the roommate, but he'd heard plenty of stories about him as he and Jared had shared a drink at Nate's bar.

"Hi," Felix said, and raised a hand.

"Uh, yes. Hello." Jared's roommate's voice was as stiff as his body.

"Ignore Ethan," Jared said from behind Felix, and squeezed Felix's shoulders. "His brain is so full of research; he forgets how to socialize with human beings sometimes."

Felix quirked an eyebrow. "Right." He folded his jacket over his arm.

The previously unreadable expression on Ethan's face quickly turned to one of embarrassment as he grimaced and turned to face the wall.

"Have you eaten?" Jared asked, guiding him to the empty seat on the couch beside Ethan.

Felix sat, glancing at the back of Ethan's head, his attention drawn to where his blond hair met the collar of his shirt, a mole behind his ear.

Well, this is awkward.

"Felix?"

"Oh, dinner?" He looked up at Jared. "Not yet. I'll eat when I get home."

"You sure? There'll be plenty. It's Ethan's mom's special casserole recipe."

At the sound of his name, Ethan turned and met Felix's eyes. He flashed a smile. "It's good."

Felix returned his smile, something tightening in his chest at the hope and happiness in Ethan's stunning blue eyes. He didn't recall Jared mentioning that Ethan was cute and had beautiful eyes. Hell, Felix would have remembered that. He cleared his throat and recalled he'd been asked a question about food.

"Maybe another time. I really can't stay long." He leaned forward, waiting for Jared to get comfy on a large beanbag before asking, "So what is it you wanted to talk about?" He clasped his hands together.

Jared shrugged. "It's nothing much. It's just a small, tiny favor."

"What kind of favor?"

"As I said. Small." He held up his hand, his index finger and thumb close to each other. "The thing is"— *This is going to be something I don't like, isn't it?*—"Ethan is going to his school reunion next week."

Felix narrowed his eyes. "Uh huh?"

"I am," Ethan stated. "With a plus-one."

Am I supposed to care? He vaguely remembered Jared telling tales of his roommate's numerous boyfriends and the ridiculous antics he got up to. Felix's favorite story ended with a purple-dyed police officer. He didn't know who Ethan was dating now, but good for him if it was going well.

"And you're telling me this because?"

"Well…" Ethan bit his lower lip, rolling his eyes upward as he seemed to process his words before speaking. There was something more sexy than cute about the way he tugged on his soft pink lips with his teeth.

He should stop doing that—he'll end up bruising them, and they're too pretty to be bruised.

Unless it's me kissing them and… the fuck?

"Well, Ethan's plus-one kind of did him dirty." Jared answered for him. "Ethan got dumped. Again," he added straight-faced.

"I dumped him," Ethan said in a strained voice.

Jared met Felix's eyes and shook his head. "He didn't," he mouthed.

Felix snorted a laugh, but his smile faded as the *favor* Jared had in mind hit him front and center. "No," he said.

"I've said nothing," Jared said, blinking with all the innocence he could muster.

Felix ran his hand back through his bangs. "I know what you're going to ask, and the answer is no." He leaned back, side-eyeing Ethan. "Why don't you ask Caleb? He'll take anything you can throw at him."

"Well, of course, I tried him first, but he's already booked. But we all know you're the best person for the job, and you owe me one."

"Well, you don't need me." Felix directed this at

Ethan. "There's nothing wrong with going alone. I'm sure there'll be plenty of people without partners."

Jared and Ethan exchanged a glance Felix couldn't decipher. Ethan opened his mouth, hesitated, then said, "But—"

"He already plus-one'd," Jared interrupted.

Felix was puzzled. "Surely he can un-plus-one himself. Problem solved." Being single wasn't a bad thing. "Look, I really need to get back home. My dad…" He went to stand, but Ethan grabbed his wrist, pulling him back to the cushion.

"Please," Ethan said.

Felix stared at Ethan's hand, raising his eyes until he met Ethan's gaze.

"Sorry," Ethan said, and withdrew.

"Come on," Jared tried. "You do owe me."

I know I do.

Jared shuffled awkwardly to get on his knees on the beanbag. "I know you've a lot going on, but it's only one night. I promise. The place is like an hour out from here, plus Ethan's great at making excuses to leave social gatherings early. Aren't you?" He nodded in Ethan's direction.

Ethan nodded, with a little too much enthusiasm.

Is that really something to be proud of?

Felix sighed and stared at Jared. He tilted his head as he realized something. "Wait. Why can't *you* do it?"

"Him?" Ethan said in horror.

"Yes, him." Felix jabbed the air in Jared's direction.

"No way," Jared said. "I get chills just thinking about it."

"Charming." Ethan pouted and folded his arms across his chest.

Jared shook his head. "No, I mean we're friends. It'd be way too weird to pretend to be in love with him." He smiled. "And I already promised Luka I'd uhm… take him to see a movie."

"That particular night."

"The only showing," Jared said—he was clearly lying. "Anyway, I thought Bryant and Waites' number one boyfriend for hire would be perfect for the job."

Number one? In my dreams.

"We both know that isn't true." Jared and Ethan stared at him expectantly. "I appreciate the flattery, but even if I say yes, I'm not sure I feel okay doing this outside of office hours. If something happened, I…"

He didn't know what that something might be, but the last thing he wanted was to do anything that might reflect badly on the company, or Gideon himself, when Gideon had been so understanding of Felix's situation with his parents.

"Nothing will happen."

"I can't," Felix said.

Ethan jolted upright, and with confidence said, "I'll pay you." He raised a finger to his mouth, nibbled the tip of his fingernail before deflating and sinking back into his seat. "Though friends and family rates would be greatly appreciated."

Though Felix wouldn't say no to some extra cash, it wasn't whether he'd get paid that he had a problem with.

"It's not about the money. I don't feel right doing a

boyfriend job off the books. It feels… I don't know. Disrespectful?" To both Gideon and the company, and the fact that Gideon had been so good about his time off. "It's nothing against you, Ethan." He met Ethan's gaze. "It really isn't." Under different circumstances, he would've agreed to work with Ethan and figured it would be fun to get to know more about the roommate Jared had described. Maybe get to see what lay beyond the stories of a ridiculous science nerd who inhabited his own little universe and was unlucky in love.

"What you're saying is, you'll do it if I okay it through Rowan?" Jared grinned.

"Am I?" Felix glanced at Ethan whose expression had brightened. "I didn't say—"

"Perfect," Jared said. "It's a deal."

Felix opened and closed his mouth, trying to figure out how to argue against their sudden enthusiasm. He looked from Ethan to Jared, each giving the other a high five from a distance.

Jared rolled off the beanbag and jumped up to his feet. "Where's my phone?"

"Dining table," Ethan said.

"What are you doing?" Felix was confused as to how they had gotten to this point.

"Calling Rowan."

Felix blinked. "Right now?"

"Yep." Jared dipped out of the room to collect his phone.

"Seriously?" Felix uttered.

"Seriously." Jared flashed him a smile on his return and thumbed the screen of his cell phone.

Felix felt exhausted. "You're messing with me—"

"Hi, Rowan," Jared said and sat on the arm of the couch next to Ethan. "Can I run something past you?"

Felix didn't have the energy to protest. He sat back, hugged the jacket in his lap, and tuned out of the one-sided conversation.

What the hell just happened?

Chapter Two

"He didn't want to do it," Ethan said as soon as the door shut behind a confused Felix. He slumped back on the sofa, scrubbing at his face as if he could wipe away the burning embarrassment. Did Jared have to mention what had happened with Darren? Every time Ethan broke up with a guy, Jared had something to say, and he was only joking, and it wasn't malicious, because Jared had his back. But... the gentlest of teasing reminded him how shit he was at balancing his life—or worse, picking men—and how he didn't even try if he was with someone, and how in the end, they all left him. Or he didn't notice they were married, or psychotic, or immature.

Jared, wearing his psychologist hat, suggested that the reason Ethan had such a hard time with relationships came down to issues of emotional vulnerability. Ethan disagreed—there was nothing wrong with his emotions or his vulnerability or whatever. He either didn't care enough about the guys he met, or he cared too much, and he couldn't find that middle ground. With a pretend boyfriend, he wouldn't need to worry about finding the middle ground, he could just be himself.

"It'll be fine." Jared ruffled Ethan's hair as he walked past to the tiny kitchen.

"It won't," Ethan muttered to himself. In what universe was it going to be fine for him going on a fake Christmas date with the gorgeous and unattainable Felix? He could imagine the mess he'd make of everything while dealing with whatever school nonsense he had to wade through. "I still don't know why I have to go to this stupid thing."

Jared came back with two beers and passed one to Ethan.

"You know why."

"I know why *you* think it's important." He left off outright saying he didn't agree, because he worked very hard on his friendship with Jared, and he always listened to him.

"Things happened to you at school, E," Jared said with a sigh. "And again, if we can get to the root of it—"

"So, I go there with my fake boyfriend, and what? I convince everyone I won at life, and suddenly, all the bad stuff is done. Do you really think that one night meeting up with people I don't even remember is really going to change anything about me?"

Jared curled up next to him on the sofa and stared at him for a while—long enough for Ethan to squirm. He didn't want to be analyzed, he *just* wanted to do his work, save the world by creating unlimited sustainable energy, learn how to cook, and get a normal boyfriend. Not necessarily in that order.

"I don't know for sure," Jared began. "But I have a good feeling that refreshing your memory of your high school life might banish some old ghosts."

"And then I'll be able to have a normal healthy relationship that I won't fuck up?"

Jared smiled. "It's a start."

Coffee N' Cookies was Ethan's second favorite place in New York. His first love would always be the laboratories at the university, but this was close behind. It was the only place, in his opinion, that sold the perfect white chocolate cookie with the flawless balance of chocolate, and a chewy texture that was also the right side of crumbly. Baking was alchemy of the highest standard and worrying about Felix arriving any minute would not ruin this morning's commune with the gods of caffeine and chocolate.

I can do this. I can talk to the hot guy for however long it takes. I will not ask inappropriate questions; I will not make a fool of myself.

Sleep had been a long time coming last night, and despite repeating the periodic table over and over, it was almost four by the time he'd dozed off. His alarm blaring at seven was a shock not even three of the strongest coffees could counteract, and now, on top of all that, he was meeting the man who was going to pretend to be his boyfriend.

Why am I doing this? Why is he *doing this?*

When he'd explained his current dilemma to Jared, he'd imagined his best friend would tell him not to bother going to the reunion, but no. He was all about Ethan confronting these alleged ghosts and making peace with his past, or some nonsense Jared had explained in depth on more than one occasion. At least, that is what Ethan assumed Jared had been doing all three times, because on each occasion, he'd stopped listening halfway through. Not deliberately, but it had occurred to him the last time that maybe the missing element in his current work was one he hadn't thought of before, and he'd spent the last part of Jared's speech wavering between beryllium and calcium.

Of course, Jared had gotten exasperated with him, but they'd hugged it out, and then, at the end of the last speech, Jared had called Felix—sexy, sultry, confident but confused Felix—and bartered a solution to Ethan's issue. Objectively, Ethan knew most people went to reunions because they had things to say to people, things to prove. But when he'd accepted the invite and added a plus-one, he'd done it with confidence because he'd been in a relationship with Darren—or maybe it had been Henry—either way, he'd fancied himself in forever love, and at that point, he'd felt as if he could take on the world.

So much for Henry or Darren, or the married asshole before them, because whatever the equation was for being lucky in love, Ethan hadn't solved it. In his head, it was a simple equivalence. He met someone, there was a spark, sex was had and enjoyed, and that became love, but he knew he was missing a variable—

the elusive thing that made the equation complete. Even if Jared never tired of telling him this was the wrong way to look at things, unless someone sat down and showed him the true equation for love, with at maximum a one percent tolerance, then he was at a loss.

His cell vibrated with a message from Jared. *Talk of the devil.*

Jared: *Good luck*

Ethan: *There's no such thing as luck. I don't like this.*

Jared: *Which is why you need to try*

Ethan: *You could call and cancel him*

Jared: *No, I can't*

Ethan: *I hate you.*

Jared: *I love you, too.*

. . .

With a huff, Ethan pocketed his phone and ignored the next vibration, which he hypothesized was Jared explaining how this was going to be good for Ethan.

The door opened—the twelfth person coming in since he'd sat down—and Felix walked in. For a moment, Ethan worried he was going to swallow his tongue. Nothing had changed since last night. Felix was still gorgeous, and confident, and comfortable in his own skin. His dark gaze scanned the shop, and *fuck*, he smiled when he spotted Ethan.

Ethan sketched a wave and half stood, but Felix made a hand gesture to show he was getting a coffee and then, pointed at him, which Ethan guessed was him asking if he wanted one? Ethan held up his cup to show him he was okay, then Felix sauntered to the counter. After five slow minutes, when all Ethan could do was stare at Felix's ass in snug-fitting jeans, his new fake date headed over to the table and took the chair opposite.

"Morning," Felix said, removing his outdoor clothes before taking a seat and blowing on his coffee. Ethan blinked at him—watching his lips as he blew—and noted the way his tongue darted out to collect some of the foam as it neared the edge of the cup. Neither of those things on their own were sexy, but added together with his eyes, and his ass, and his smile, he was a potent package. Ethan had the worrying thought that he was more than just a little attracted to Felix.

Danger.

This whole date thing *wasn't* about Ethan experimenting with Jared's coworker. It was a simple transaction, not kisses and sex and potential falling in love on day one, or even finding the elusive thing that could make his love life work, and he had to remain calm.

"Morning," Ethan began with purpose, then couldn't think of anything else to say. The deep brown of Felix's eyes was a mix between amber and something else. *What else?* His head spun with the possibilities of replicating that shade, and he considered how he might achieve that in the university laboratories. *But to get the dark brown with the amber, I'd need what?*

"—some backstory."

"Huh?"

Felix had his head tilted as if he was trying to solve a puzzle and not quite understanding the clues. Then he straightened and cleared his throat.

"I was just saying that we should establish what you need from me, and I have some questions that might help."

Stop thinking about his eyes. "Okay," Ethan murmured, and then squirmed a little. "I get it's not something you really wanted to do. I understand Jared forced you into a corner, but there's a reason I need to go to this thing. Although, I don't fully appreciate what the reason is, or I mean, I understand that objectively I need to close doors, or that's what Jared says. Not real doors, of course, metaphorical doors that are open and letting in a figurative draft that cools down the rest of my life." He sighed. "That made no sense, did it?"

"I kind of get it," Felix said, though Ethan guessed that was a lie.

"Well, it sounded good in my head, but Jared will tell

you I can go off at a tangent and then, people can't follow what I mean. Like, right now, all I can think about is amber, which leads to the word Jurassic—the implausible movie with the dinosaurs I mean, not the actual era itself. All of that naturally moves into the considerations for reconstructing ancient proteins to design optimal biocatalysts for the future."

Ethan sat back in his chair, acutely aware he'd just dumped a ton of nonsense onto the table, and Felix was now left to pick his way through it.

"Naturally," Felix agreed after a short pause. Then he cleared his throat. "So, how about we start small? Talk about the event itself."

Ethan fidgeted as he listed off the inert gases in his head to center himself. Talking wasn't his strong point, which was why meeting guys went from zero to blowjobs in less than five minutes—he couldn't ramble on if he had a cock in his mouth.

"It's a ten-year reunion, which… I mean, who even has those?"

Felix quirked an eyebrow.

"Yeah, you're right. Ten is a thing, isn't it? But I mean, shouldn't it be longer? Let people actually do something with their lives. Maybe go with twenty years, or thirty. It's ridiculous that people want to meet up after ten. I mean, it's ten. That's not long at all, right?"

Felix nodded and pulled out a notebook, a pocket-sized leather-bound journal and the smallest of pens that hooked to the side. "So, we'd be attending a school reunion."

"Yep. Ten years."

He ignored Ethan and forged ahead. "What type of school was it?"

Ethan searched his databank for an appropriate answer. "It had students, and a football team, and the labs were okay, I guess, although the chemistry teacher had very limited expectations of what we could or *should* be doing."

Felix didn't make a note of that. "I meant more, public or private, that kind of thing."

"Oh, private. I had a scholarship though, so don't think I have money, because I don't."

"Friend's rates, I remember," Felix said with a smile.

Another flare of attraction erupted somewhere inside Ethan, which he ruthlessly pushed down.

"Yeah, so. Right." *Words, where are you?*

"So, tell me a bit more about what to expect."

"Quiche, I imagine, tiny fancy ones you don't even have to chew."

Felix snorted a laugh, but Ethan wasn't sure what he'd said that was funny.

"Mini quiche got it. But I was thinking more along the lines of what about your friends and their expectations of our relationship status?"

Ethan analyzed the question and wondered how he was going to answer it. "I didn't have many friends. Or rather, I had exactly one. Julian," he finally offered. "But I had lab partners and shared a lunch table with Julian who had this unfortunate… thing." He indicated his face and then, grimaced.

"Will Julian be there?"

"I have no idea."

"Can you check his social media?"

Ethan blinked. "*His* social media? How would I do that?" Ethan had accounts on a couple of platforms out of a feeling of obligation and it being the expected thing for a teenager off to college, but that didn't mean he'd touched them in years, or even knew what to do with them.

"Okay, I'll work with what I've got," Felix said after a pause. "Anyone else aside from Julian with the 'unfortunate *thing*'?"

Ethan narrowed his gaze, but Felix didn't appear to be teasing him. It was more a statement of fact.

"Not really. I was more into studying than socializing. There were some people who would talk to me. Acquaintances would be the word for them." Ethan quirked a smile.

"Okay," Felix repeated, then changed the subject. "So, these metaphorical open doors you mentioned, what part is attending the reunion going to play in shutting them?"

"I don't call them doors, Jared does, but he's studying psychology and always tries to get me to recognize myself in terms of things I'll understand. If only he used chemical equations, we wouldn't be having half the issues we do. Or the kind of term they use on the Discovery Channel. I enjoy watching documentaries there. Nat Geo, too—all those different animals and the interesting way they structure the world, so different from ours. Just the other day I—"

"And back to the open doors?"

"Oh yeah, sorry." Ethan pressed fingers to his mouth

and tapped them to stop the words from falling out so fast. It grounded him when words were being hard. Finally, he was centered enough to concentrate. "So, Jared says that I can't have a healthy relationship because I have open doors. One for my work, another for school, one for family, another one for... I forget. So, I'm going to this reunion to find whatever door I left open there, and I'm going to close it. Metaphorically. Not a real door."

"I get the concept," Felix said with a smile.

"You do? That's more than I do then. So, what else do you need to know?"

"Let's start with the event itself, black-tie or costume party? I'm guessing as it's in November that is has a Christmas theme. Or a snow theme?"

"It's called the Snow Ball," Ethan offered. He remembered that much from the invitation. "So, fancy dresses and things. Not for us, although if you like to wear dresses, then that is cool with me. I tried a dress once, and it was comfortable, but..." Ethan stopped and dipped his gaze, aware he'd gone off on a tangent. "Sorry, carry on."

"It's okay. I get you're worrying, and it's my job to take that worry away. So, how about you forward the invitation to me, and we can take it from there?"

"Okay."

By the time the coffee meeting was over, Felix had a page of notes, and Ethan had a headache.

But at least, between them, they had a plan.

Chapter Three

"Dad?" Felix took a step back from the full-length mirror and stared through the gap in the door. "Dad," he called again. His gaze settled on an old teddy bear sitting on a chair in the corner of the room. Its nose bore a balding patch, and its body was squashed, the stuffing flattened from too many hugs.

I really loved that thing, huh?

He had moved out almost ten years ago, and the room was no longer something he'd call his, and yet, there was still evidence of his childhood tucked away in the corners—photographs, trophies, toys. One closet was still half-filled with some of his old clothes. He glanced down, breathing in as he ran his hand over his stomach. He'd turned thirty at the start of the year, and though he didn't think he'd changed all that much since his twenties, he wondered if anything he wore back then would still fit him. He checked himself out in the mirror, jumping as his door flew open with a thump against the wood, and his dad walked in.

"What?" His dad wore a frown, resting his good arm on the tall dresser by the door.

"Okay, Mr. Grumps," Felix teased. "Just wanted to remind you about supper being in the refrigerator. Oh, and leave the dishes. I'll tidy up when I come by in the morning." He turned back to the mirror, raising his chin as he turned down his collar.

"Again? You don't have to do that." He raised his injured arm. "I can manage a few dishes." Felix had been staying between his parents' place and his own since his dad's fall.

Charlie Ryan, as stubborn as ever.

"Oh, really."

His dad cursed under his breath.

"So, may I keep the car then?" He hadn't been able to rely on Rowan to organize transport this time because it wasn't an official job, so he was using his dad's car for the night. He didn't mind, he wasn't much of a drinker anyway; plus, it made things easier when Ethan called time on his reunion efforts and door-closing or whatever, and it was time to leave.

Huffing a breath, Charlie curled down his bottom lip. "Fine. Do what you want. You usually do anyway."

"And where do you think he gets it from?" Karin tapped her husband's backside as she rolled up behind him. She smiled up at Charlie, melting away his frown. "His good looks, too."

Felix leaned over to kiss his mom's cheek.

"You look very handsome." She reached up and straightened his tie. "Is it for work?"

"It's more a favor for a friend."

"Friend?"

He met his mother's eyes. She tilted her head, a smile spreading across her face as her interest was piqued.

"*Just* a friend. Or rather a friend of a friend," he added, then regretted it as his mom's eyes flickered from disappointed to hopeful. "Mom," he warned.

"Let me dream," Karin said. She gripped his hand, rubbing her thumb over the back of his hand. "You know I just want to see you happy."

"Mom."

"I know. I know." She let go of him. "You *are* happy. You're all grown up and can look after yourself."

There was an ache in his chest. He knew she was alluding to a recent conversation they'd had—the fact they were getting older, both in their seventies. Age hadn't meant anything to him as a kid, the fact his parents had ten, twenty years on his friends' parents. His mom was worried about him. Who would he have to do that once they were gone?

"I *am* happy." Or at least he was happier than he had been in his last serious relationship. Had it really been three years since he'd split from Nolan? He hadn't had a long-term relationship since then, nobody he'd gotten around to introducing to his parents as a *boyfriend*. Honestly, he didn't care about being single. The sense of freedom after years of feeling as if he was being suffocated had been refreshing.

He kissed his mom again and reassured her by saying, "I promise."

She nodded and rested her hands in her lap. "You should get going. You don't want to be late."

Felix checked his watch. "You're right. I'm staying at my place tonight as I have no idea what time I'll be back. I'll drop the car back in the morning and"—he looked at his father and pointed at him—"I'll do the dishes then, too."

"Fine. Just go already."

Felix chuckled and grabbed his jacket off the bed.

"Have fun," Karin said.

He shrugged on his suit jacket. "I'll try my best."

Maybe it won't be as bad as I think.

"Hey," Felix called out, jogging to where Ethan stood outside his building. "Made it. Were you waiting long?"

Ethan shook his head, and his normally tousled blond hair was styled so his bangs were combed back from his face. "Based on the time you sent your text and where you'd said your parents lived and the traffic at this time, I made a sensible estimate of when you'd arrive."

"Really?"

"No. I just got lucky. Until a minute ago, I was wandering around my apartment panicking about several things, like whether I'd forgotten something. Or was the date of the reunion actually tonight, or whether I should call it all off, stay home, and go through my research data while consuming the half-gallon of mint choc chip ice cream Jared bought last week." He tapped his lips. "I mean, he wouldn't notice anything for up to a couple of months. He stays with Nate most of the time.

Only really keeps paying his share of the rent so he's got somewhere kid-free and quiet to study."

Snorting a laugh, Felix suggested, "Before you talk yourself out of going, should we go to the car and head out?"

"Would it be such a bad thing if I did decide not to go?"

Felix shrugged. "I have no idea. I'm not the one who'll have to explain to Jared about all his doors still being wide open." He wasn't fully on board with whatever analogy Jared had sold Ethan with all this door talk, but he kind of understood it. He knew that some relationships and connections—doors—needed to be closed and moved on from.

"You make a good point. To the reunion." Ethan headed in the direction Felix had approached from.

Felix chuckled, watching him for a few steps, until Ethan stopped and glanced over his shoulder.

"Uh. Where did you park?"

Certainly, from Jared's tales, it seemed as if Ethan acted on impulse, especially when his emotions were in disarray. Felix smiled and came to Ethan's side. "Come on." He rested his hand on Ethan's shoulder. "And try to relax. Tonight, will be fine. I mean, it's not all bad, right?

"It isn't?" Ethan raised his thin eyebrows.

"Of course not." Felix pressed his hand to his chest. "You've got me."

Ethan opened his mouth and seemed surprised. Then, he dipped his gaze. "Thanks," he said, shyly.

They both fell silent and beneath his palm, Felix

could feel the heavy thump of his heart. He'd said what he did to give Ethan courage, but the words left him with an uneasy feeling, having seen the brightening of Ethan's expression and eyes.

Had he crossed the line and said something he shouldn't have? Or rather, was he feeling something he shouldn't?

That same brightness in Ethan's features had ignited a spark of curiosity in Felix. Ethan was handsome, funny, endearing, and by all accounts, oblivious to all of it. Felix guessed a string of failed relationships could probably dull someone to their own qualities.

Just like me.

"Felix?"

Felix blinked and realized he'd been staring straight through Ethan to God knows where. "Sorry. Miles away."

"I'm feeling a bit better about tonight." He nodded ahead of them. "I'm good, so shall we?"

With a smile, Felix said, "Let's."

They used the drive to go over some of the details of their *relationship*. Simple was always best, as far as Felix was concerned.

"Okay, so one last time. First meeting?" Felix asked.

"I literally bumped into you at my favorite coffee shop. Spilled your drink and offered to buy you another."

"My job?"

"Definitely not a rentable boyfriend."

"Sure, but maybe don't say that."

Ethan rested his elbow on the car door. "As if I would."

"So? My job?" Felix prompted again.

"Freelance programmer." Ethan chewed on his fingernail. "Just out of curiosity, why?"

Felix puffed his cheeks and blew a breath. "Freelance means there's no company name getting thrown about, and believe it or not, I studied software engineering for a few years. Your favor was a little short notice for a deep dive on a background in something else, so if anyone decides to be a nosey smartass, I can hold my own to a degree."

Ethan exhaled through his nose. "Clever."

"I figured it was easier this way. They say something about keeping your lies based on truths, don't they?" They passed a sign saying their exit was coming up. "Nearly there," he pointed out and signaled.

"Great," Ethan said on a sigh. "Staying at home with that ice cream suddenly seems like a better idea after all."

"It's too late to wimp out now, I'm afraid." Felix took the turn toward the Marlow St. James Estate. He knew a little about the place where the reunion was being held, some fancy place that rented out event spaces for anything from fifteen to three hundred people. Yesterday, he and Jared had met with Rowan to get the final okay on the unofficial *boyfriend date*, and apparently, Bryant and Waites had taken on a client for a wedding job there a couple of years back.

Ethan fell silent for the last stretch of their journey,

and it wasn't until they pulled up in a parking bay that he let out a huffed breath and a strained sound.

Felix turned off the engine and sat back in his seat. He stared out the window, listening as Ethan muttered a few words of encouragement to himself.

"It's going to be fine." Ethan hesitated, scratching behind his ear. "Fine." Taking a breath, he opened the car door and, after a moment, stepped out.

Felix followed. He watched from over the top of the car, smiling as Ethan continued to cheer himself on toward the entrance. He pushed his door shut and walked around to the passenger side.

"Hey," Felix said and caught Ethan's hand.

Ethan checked around. There were a few other people milling between the cars, probably having just arrived themselves. "Is this okay?" He turned his wrist but didn't break free of Felix's hold.

"You've brought your *boyfriend* with you, right? I think it's a little late to worry about anyone seeing us holding hands."

"I know. I guess—"

Felix loosened his grip. "But if you're not comfortable, we can skip the PDA."

"No." Ethan grabbed him more tightly. "It's not as if they don't know I'm gay. They all told me I was, long before I even thought about it myself." He swallowed hard and Felix wondered what it had been like for Ethan to be out at high school.

I skipped that experience.

"Screw it and screw anyone who disapproves,"

Ethan blurted out. He pulled Felix forward as his pace quickened and he marched to the doors.

The building was more modern than Felix had imagined, all white and glass and angular, a contrast to the rustic and wooden charm that had sprung to mind when Rowan had mentioned the location being used for a wedding.

"Welcome to Marlowe St. James," a well-spoken blonde greeted them inside. She was all teeth as she smiled and glanced between the two of them. "I'm Denise. How can I help?"

"Hi. We're here for the reunion," Ethan said stiffly and squeezed Felix's hand.

Felix glanced past the staff member to the board behind her. It seemed there was at least one other function room in use that evening.

"Great. If you head to the right." She explained to Ethan where he needed to go. "Someone will greet you when you get there."

"Thanks." Ethan led Felix by the hand, flashing the woman a polite smile and heading in the direction she had told him.

Felix squeezed his hand. "You doing okay?" he asked.

"I'm fine." He slowed his pace a little. "Sorry. Unfamiliar things, places, people, kind of put me on edge." He let out a steady breath. "I'll calm down once I get in there and settled and…" He glanced over at Felix. "Thank you for being here."

"Sure."

They stepped through a large pair of French doors and were greeted by a young woman.

"Hello," she said with a smile. "You are...?" She narrowed her eyes and checked between the two of them, and then down at a list that rested on the table behind which she was standing.

"Ethan Cooper."

Felix would have been offended on his behalf at her lack of recognition, but from their conversation in the coffee shop, he doubted Ethan had a clue who the lady in front of them was either. If he thought about it, he doubted he could name, or even recognize many people who'd been his classmates in high school. Props to this lady for pretending she stood a chance to get Ethan's name.

Ethan squeezed Felix's hand. "And this is Felix, my plus-one."

"I'm Ada. Nice to meet you."

"Same," Felix said.

She handed Ethan a name badge, then directed him into the function room. An explosion of blue and silver, a million fairy lights, and a disco ball in the center were an assault to the senses when they stepped inside.

"That wasn't so bad," Felix said in a low voice as he slipped off his suit jacket. He smiled as Ethan copied him before fixing his tie, noting the pale pink shirt that had a delicate paisley design in silver, completed with the navy bow tie matching the shade of his dress pants.

"Did you tie that yourself?" Felix rested his jacket over his arm and scanned the room.

Ethan grinned, then turned his back and lifted his

collar. "No." He met Felix's eyes over his shoulder. "Disappointed?"

Felix noted the clasp and shook his head. "Not at all."

They stepped down into the room that had been set up with several large circular tables for guests. There was a bar at the far side of the room, as well as serving counters for food later that evening. The smell of pine from three huge Christmas trees filled the air, so much so that Felix assumed there was an air freshener, or ten, set to blast out eau-de-pine at intervals.

"Wow." Felix eyed the decorations hanging around the large space. There were various shades of blue and silver sparkle, and Christmas arrangements on tables and hanging on walls and from the ceiling, and more strings of fairy lights than Felix cared to count. "That's something."

"It is kind of pretty," Ethan said.

So many lights.

"Hello," a cheery voice said from behind them. "Ethan. Drink?"

Felix suddenly found himself with a flute of something fizzy and, from the taste of it—alcoholic—in his hand.

"Dolly," Ethan said.

So, he does know some *names?*

"You look very handsome," Dolly said. "So does your... boyfriend?"

"Felix," Felix introduced himself. "And yes, boyfriend."

"That's really great." She balanced the tray of

drinks in one hand so she could hold up her left, light catching the stone on the ring she wore. "Simon proposed last month while we were vacationing in Cabo San Lucas."

"Congratulations," Ethan said.

"Thank you. Anyway, I need to go hand these out. We should catch up properly later. See you." She winked at Felix, then left.

When she was out of earshot, he leaned in close to Ethan. "You know Dolly?"

"Who would forget someone called Dolly," Ethan murmured.

"And who's Simon?"

"I don't know," he whispered.

Felix covered his mouth as he held back a laugh.

"Ugh," Ethan said and glanced around. "What am I even doing here…" His gaze lingered on one table at the far side of the room. An indescribable expression passed over his face.

Had he seen someone he knew?

Felix eyed the group of men sitting at the table. Maybe one of them was the friend he'd mentioned before. Julian, with the face thing, if he remembered correctly.

Out of nowhere, Ethan downed his drink. "Where'd Dolly go? I could really go for another glass."

"Do you want mine? I'm driving so…"

Ethan exchanged his empty glass with Felix's and, immediately, tilted his head back and drained the glass.

"Hey. You should go easy," Felix advised.

"Why?" There was an edge to Ethan's tone.

"It's up to you, but for one, I thought you came here to close some doors, not fall ass-first through them."

Ethan glanced from his empty glass to the group around the table.

"Two, I don't really want to have to explain to Jared why I let his roommate come home drunk as hell."

"Jared isn't home tonight. Wasn't yesterday, and likely won't be tomorrow."

Felix sighed. "That's not the—"

"I know. I get it." He held the empty glass out to Felix. "Point taken," he said in a soft voice. "I guess I still feel a little weird about this whole reunion thing."

Felix took the glass. He pinched the rims together and held the pair of glasses by his side.

With a huff, Ethan stretched his neck from side to side and straightened his bow tie. He relaxed his shoulders and touched Felix's forearm. "How about we go find me a soda or something instead? Then we can mingle."

Was everything okay? Felix resisted questioning Ethan about the brief change in his mood as, for the time being, it seemed he was back to normal. Or what Felix judged as Ethan's normal from their brief time together.

"There's a patio with heaters. We could get some fresh air," Ethan added.

Felix took hold of Ethan's hand and gave it a squeeze.

He was going to be okay, right?

Chapter Four

A marquee over the patio kept the worst of the weather from anyone who stood outside, and the heaters were on full blast. Out here was almost a mirror image of what was inside, all blue and silver, but without the disco ball. There were a few tables with chairs, with blankets over the back of each one. Ethan could see through the plastic siding that there was a group of hardy smokers clustered outside. He wondered if they were the same people who used to hide behind the sports block back in school. He bit his lip when the instinct to explain his theories on smoking were about to spill out—he didn't think Felix would want to hear that right now.

"I'll get you a drink. What would you like?" Felix asked.

Ethan was so determined not to let his mouth run away with him that he didn't give his usual explanation of how he tried to avoid beer because it made his head spin. Felix didn't need to know that either. He should probably act cool, right?

"Surprise me."

Felix raised an eyebrow, as if that very concept worried him.

"I don't want to get you the wrong thing. After all, if you read the small print you would have seen that I'm a thoughtful boyfriend."

"Wait. I didn't sign a contract. Should I have signed a contract? Am I liable for anything? Shit, I should have got Jared to check the small print. I'm an idiot."

Felix placed a hand on his chest to stop him. "No, there wasn't really a contract with small print. This is off the books, right? You understand that you're not liable for anything."

"But, in reality, what if there's an accident?"

"You mean if the disco ball falls on our heads?"

Ethan peered past Felix but couldn't see the disco ball from here. "Did you notice it was loose? I've seen that happen in movies. People killed by falling disco balls. Particularly, if there's an earthquake."

"I didn't order an earthquake tonight, that's only included as part of our disaster package," Felix deadpanned. "So, there will not be an earthquake, the disco ball won't fall on top of anyone, and I'm never going to get you a drink that you haven't specifically chosen. That's all in the unofficial small print."

"You have a disaster package?" Ethan blinked at him, feeling as if Felix had just made a really cool joke, and wondering if it might be appropriate for him to laugh, and if so, what kind of laugh? Was it a chuckle situation, or maybe a belly laugh. He knew Felix was trying to take his mind off what they were here to do, but he didn't feel like laughing. Instead, all he felt was a strange pull to run screaming in the opposite direction of whatever version of Hell this reunion was.

"It's extra if you want an upside-down boat."

"A what now?"

"Like in the movie *The Poseidon Adventure*, not the new one, the original."

"I don't think I've seen that one."

"An ocean liner gets hit with a rogue wave and is turned upside down." Felix explained the move with his hands.

"They should have turned the boat, so they met the wave bow-first. The captain should have known that?"

"It's a uh… movie…" Felix said.

"Uhmm…" Ethan knew he'd lost the thread of whatever joke Felix had started. "Can I get a Jack and Coke?" he asked after staring into Felix's amber eyes and focusing hard.

"Is that a question or an order," Felix teased, and underscored it by adding an encouraging smile.

"Oh, sorry. It's an order. But maybe the real Coke, not diet please, if that's okay."

"Good choice. Have a seat, and I'll be right back." Felix even pressed a kiss to Ethan's hair, and side-hugged him—the sort of simple PDA that would make anybody watching think they were together. Felix was very good at his job, it seemed.

Also, true to his word, he was there and back at the table in three minutes and twenty-nine seconds—clearly, there wasn't a line for alcohol at the moment. He placed the drinks on the table, then tucked a blanket around

Ethan's knees before taking a seat opposite him. The Jack and Coke slipped down a treat, and before Ethan knew it, the glass was empty.

Wow, that went fast. Maybe it was a small one?

"I'm guessing you don't want to stay out here all night," Felix asked, nursing his sparkling water and half smiling as he waited for an answer.

In reality, all Ethan wanted to do was sit out here, with Felix, a steady supply of Jack and Coke, and maybe some nibbles. Those metaphorical doors of his might well stay open, but at least he wouldn't have any messy confrontations with specters from his past. He was cozy under the blanket, his face toasty warm, and he had one of the sexiest men he'd ever seen sitting in front of him. Part of him didn't want this to end. He wasn't sure if it was because he was a coward, or whether he felt at peace for the first time since he'd received the invite and Jared had persuaded him he needed to attend.

"I want to stay right here. With you. But that would defeat the object of being here."

"True, and there's music back in there, and a cocktail bar where you can learn how to make your own cocktails. We could have a dance, make a cocktail, see if anybody steps through your open doors?"

Ethan ignored the doors part of that sentence. "I can dance, at least I think I can, in that I know how it works. I'm just not sure I'm sexy enough to have anything more than a shuffle around the floor. I can't do any dipping or anything like that. No jumps."

Felix nodded in all seriousness. "There goes my *Dirty Dancing* idea."

Ethan knew *that* was a joke, and he chuckled. "I've never seen that movie, but I understand the cultural reference, so that makes it funny." He knew he didn't need to say that. No one *really* wanted to hear explanations of why he thought things were funny. He was supposed to laugh and join in. Never mind. He had the rest of the evening to appear completely normal.

"It's my mom's favorite movie, she used to be a dancer, way back before…"

"Before what?"

"Oh, before nothing. Sorry, I got distracted." Ethan thought Felix seemed anything *but* distracted. Instead, he looked kind of melancholy. But then he seemed to shake it off and forged ahead. "Anyway, back to tonight. What door do we tackle first?"

Ethan wished he could identify any incident, let alone *the* one that was going to fix him as Jared said it would. His friend was adamant there was this nebulous thing in his past he'd hidden from even himself; the kind of thing that was keeping him unhappy and may be responsible for him searching for a relationship with the wrong men. For the life of him he couldn't think what it could be.

His school life was a blur of wanting to learn and study, but he had a few specific incidents that might have made a door stay open. Still, there was only one that stuck out for him, and that was the time the entire swim team had locked him in the changing rooms and stole his clothes. It was a shame really, because swimming had been the one sport he'd been any good at, but the incident *did* put him off joining in the organized sport for much longer.

Still the swim team had apologized—in a mortifying meeting outside the principal's office. Given it was the entire team, all twelve of them, it would have been difficult for everyone to fit inside the small room from where the principal lorded it over the school. Which meant there was an audience, as said principal made each member apologize in the hallway. Once the embarrassment had passed, and the school jokes died down—Ethan had amassed a collection of swimming caps nailed to his locker for a few weeks after—he felt he'd handled the situation well. It hadn't been Ethan who'd told the principal about the situation, and the team had known that, so it was done.

I swear that *door is completely shut.*

Still, it didn't stop Ethan from trying to recall the names of the team members in case he'd missed something. He got stuck on the first name, and then he realized Felix was talking to him, and heat made his cheeks burn. *Stay in the present, idiot.*

"… we go make a cocktail," Felix suggested and was smiling again—he had such a beautiful smile. Poets could probably wax lyrical about his amber eyes, and the way his long lashes feathered around them, but all Ethan could think was that Felix was a very handsome man. Also, that maybe, one day he would meet someone who smiled at him like Felix.

"Sounds like a plan," Ethan murmured after a pause, during which Felix stared at him with a curious expression.

Felix stood and extended a hand to Ethan, but right at the moment that Ethan was going to lace their fingers and never let go…

"Oh my God!" Someone yelled next to him, and Ethan started as somebody tall, dark, and built, yanked him out of his chair, and hugged him close. "Specs! I'm so pleased you're here."

Ethan eased himself away until there was a good three feet of distance. At first he didn't recognize the person who'd hugged him—gorgeous, tall, friendly, and smiling, the man looked nothing like anyone Ethan remembered from school.

Fuck. Is this my open door? Have I blocked out something that happened between us? Surely, I'd remember him being part of my world and causing me hurt?

"How have you been? Have you saved the world yet?" Gorgeous man turned to Felix and offered a hand. "Julian Cirillo. I was in Ethan's geography class. On a scholarship the same as him."

Felix and Julian exchanged pleasantries while Ethan watched in shock. This was *the* Julian with the unfortunate facial afflictions? He'd been a nice guy, they'd been friends, and he'd been an outcast the same as Ethan. Now though, his unfortunate face thing had cleared up, his teeth were straight and white, and his ears didn't stick out anymore. He'd grown into his body; whereas, Ethan knew, he'd remained a full-time member of the socially awkward club. Go figure.

"Julian." Ethan confirmed when he and Felix were done with their nice-to-meet-yous. "It's so good to see you." It *was* great to see him, because it was proof positive Ethan had memories of school that were good. Memories of laughing with Julian that could move front and center in Ethan's thoughts, forcing to one side formulas, chemical reactions, and his unfortunate appreciation of his pretend date.

"I can't call you Specs anymore." Julian waved in front of Ethan's face. "Contacts?"

Oh, a subject I can talk about.

"Yeah, I had astigmatism. That was an irregular curve in the lens or cornea of my eye, and it caused the shape to change from a circular to an oval shape. I never even realized I had it, but I went for tests, and they said I couldn't wear soft lenses, well not for this condition, so I have rigid gas-permeable lenses, which provide good eye hydration, and what I mean by that is that the lenses supply the eyes with one hundred percent of the oxygen they need."

Everything spilled out in one uncoordinated mess of information, but if Julian seemed fazed by it all, he didn't show it. If anything, it just made him smile harder. "Same old Ethan. You know, I learned so much from you."

"You did?"

"You remember when we used to sit at the same table for lunch? Us against the world. Well, we both grew up well, so that'll show them!" He gestured at his own face. "Braces, got through puberty, worked out, I'm a professional photographer, had photos in all kinds of glossy magazines."

"Like *Nat Geo*?"

"Yeah, you see that Snow Leopard spread last year around October time?"

"That was you?"

"One of my proudest moments. My husband and I work together, but that was our actual honeymoon, so I got good photos from it, and the *Nat Geo* spread was just the icing on the cake."

"Your husband?"

He seemed confused. "Remember, we were both in the closet at school? That we talked about being gay?"

"Of course," Ethan lied. "Sorry, I was making a joke," he added.

Julian rolled his eyes and snorted a laugh, as if he *actually* found Ethan funny. "I met Ben in college." Then, he poked Ethan in the chest. "But it was a good job that I didn't see you first after the crush I had on you at school." He smiled again. "I'm only joking, not about the crush, but about not meeting Ben. He's the other half of me, and I couldn't be happier. Maybe, we could meet up one day and double date? You'd like Ben. He's a math professor, all kinds of clever like you."

Ethan was lost for what to say. Julian had once had a crush on him. For real? And also, a double date? Didn't a double date rely on him having a date to bring? He wasn't sure he could afford Felix again, but, as if Felix knew Ethan was floundering, he stepped in.

"Sounds good, you should message Ethan, and we'll arrange it."

Ethan knew that was just a line Felix was using, but his chest tightened at the thought of the potential date with a man as sexy and confident as Felix.

One day.

"Anyway, can I take your photo for the event's coffee-table book?" That was when Ethan noticed the camera in Julian's hand, some fancy arrangement that looked way too technical. Ethan could explain how cameras worked, he could probably build one from parts, but taking photos wasn't in his skill set. Felix took a step back—to give Julian space, Ethan guessed—and he felt lost for a moment, wishing he could drag Felix close and hold his hand again.

"Okay," Ethan agreed. Then, he wondered if he needed to do a duck face like he'd seen in some of Jared's social media posts. Not that it was ever Jared doing the duck face. In fact, it was Nate who did the pretend pouting, and as Jared concluded in a biased fashion, because he was in love with Nate, it was Nate's pout that made every photo original.

I'm not going to do a duck face.

Julian tugged him close and held up his camera, fiddled with a button, and then suggested that Ethan smile with an enthusiastic shout of cheese.

Ethan never even got to explain why saying cheese wouldn't take a good photo, because the camera flashed, and his wide-eyed surprise was captured for eternity.

Julian side-hugged him. "Let's take another one, just for old times' sake."

Do we have to?

After two more photos, it seemed Julian deemed he had enough. "The organizers of the event hired me to take photographs, and when I say hired, I mean they suggested that, as I was attending the reunion, maybe

I'd like to take some informal snaps of people. Their words, not mine." He laughed, and Felix joined in, so Ethan smiled, and it seemed to be enough for both of them.

"Anyway, I'll tag you in the socials, but I need to get going. Maybe once I've taken everybody's photo, we could sit and have a chat?"

Julian appeared to like him, appeared to want to talk to him, and actually, it was nice.

"Of course, I'd love to."

"We'd love to," Felix interjected, side-hugged Ethan, and pressed yet another kiss to Ethan's hair. He was doing his job by staking a claim in front of someone from Ethan's past, making it seem as if Ethan had his life figured out. It seemed to work. Julian fist-bumped Ethan shook hands with Felix, and then, disappeared back into the main function room.

"Is that him?" Felix asked as soon as the coast was clear, his tone full of worry.

"Him, who?"

"Is Julian an open door? A situation to be resolved? Something that needs to be fixed?"

"No." A flood of memories wrapped around his heart. "Julian is an old friend. Someone I should have kept in touch with."

"You're sure?"

"Absolutely."

"Come on then." Felix laced their fingers and tugged Ethan in the same direction as Julian had disappeared, over to the cocktail bar that seemed to have steady business. As the mixologist explained the steps he used to create cocktails to customers' specification, all Ethan could focus on was that Julian was an example of how people had changed since school. Not only had Julian changed physically, but he seemed happy, out of the closet he'd hidden in for so long, at peace, and as if he'd found his place in the world.

Ethan was out of the closet, but there was something else messing with his head.

I could be like Julian one day.

When all my doors shut.

Chapter Five

"Say *cocktail*," Julian instructed as he focused his camera on the two of them.

Felix rested his hand on the small of Ethan's back and raised his drink. He leaned close as Julian snapped some shots of those making cocktails.

"Thank you." Julian's gaze was on Ethan as he flashed a smile. "Enjoy your drinks," he said as he left, seeming to scan the room for his next subjects.

He's married, Felix reminded himself. *Wait, what does that matter? What am I even thinking?*

Was he going to ignore the fact a sense of ownership had sprung up inside him when Julian had approached them for the second time? He was aware Ethan wasn't an object and the closeness they shared was just for show, but Felix had felt a twinge of jealousy when Julian had gotten close.

It had been a long time since he'd felt insecure, and never when he was on a job and playing pretend boyfriend.

A softness, a brightness—there had been something different about Ethan when he'd realized who Julian was and had talked with his old friend. Felix withdrew his hand from Ethan's back, stepping back to put a little space between them. He smiled as he watched Ethan create his drink, following the order and amount of ingredients with accuracy.

Ethan poured the triple sec into the measuring cylinder, then added it to the shaker along with ice, vodka, and orange juice. He waited as the mixology instructor helped him secure the two halves of the shaker before holding it tight and, with a wince of fear, probably as to whether the lid would remain in place, he started mixing his drink.

"It's so scary," Ethan said through a strained smile as he shook the container. The sound of ice and liquid sloshing together could just be made out above the music. "And my arms ache already."

Felix chuckled. Ethan didn't strike him as a gym rat, and he guessed lab work didn't make for great muscle-building. "Would you like a hand?" he offered, ready to leave his drink on the table and assist Ethan with his.

"No, no," he grumbled, raising his shoulders as he put effort into rocking the shaker vigorously. The instructor called time and the line of students poured their cocktails. "Agent Orange," Ethan mused after thanking the instructor and stepping away so others could have a go. "It has a cool name at least."

"I guess so." Felix eyed the orange and vodka-based drink. "So long as it tastes good, who cares."

"How's your Shirley Temple?" Ethan nodded

toward the glass in Felix's hand. He flicked his tongue out after sipping his own. "Wow, that's tangy." He met Felix's eyes. "So?"

"What?" Felix said, his mind had wandered, too distracted by the curve of Ethan's lips as he'd reacted to his cocktail.

"Your drink?"

"Oh right. It's fine. At least as fine as a non-alcoholic cocktail can be." He laughed. "Sounds a little sad, somehow." He held out his drink. "Did you want to try it? It's all gingery and lemony and, to be honest, I'm not sure I'd even notice the difference if they'd put alcohol in it."

Ethan shook his head. "It's fine. I'm good with this." He took another taste, once again screwing up his nose and licking his lips.

"Let's find a seat." There were no empty tables, so they ended up taking seats at a partly filled table, joining two couples and another lady who was sitting with them. After a polite greeting and compulsory making of surprised faces and sounds as if they remembered Ethan and cared who Felix was to him, the group of five returned to their own business, huddled together laughing and scanning the room, maybe reminiscing, or exchanging gossip from their high school lives.

The room had filled with more people while they had been wrapped up in cocktail-making. The blue and silver of the decorations wasn't as overbearing as before, variety had come in the form of spatters of color from the attendees and their attire. Felix glanced around. What had it been like for Ethan to attend school with these people? With a sigh, he leaned back in his seat, side-eyeing Ethan, whose attention was on something across the room.

Was it the same group of people Ethan had focused on before? He hadn't paid close attention to any faces at the time.

Ethan's expression at that moment was indecipherable, and he seemed lost in thought as he drank, not stopping until the cocktail was gone. He flinched when he tipped the glass and ice fell against his top lip. Lowering his glass, he gave a cute little pout and glanced over his shoulder at the bar.

"Do you want another? I can go get you something," Felix offered. He probably shouldn't encourage him too much, but a few cocktails wouldn't be a bad thing. Maybe help Ethan shift the last of the stress tonight had brought him.

He certainly seems more at ease. Felix glanced across the room. *Mostly.*

Ethan shook his glass until the ice lay flat, then slid his glass on the table. "Please."

"Anything in particular? Sticking to cocktails?"

Ethan breathed in and nodded. "Yeah," he said as he released his breath. "I'll have another of these. It was pretty good, if I do say so myself. Perfectly measured and mixed."

Felix nodded. "Of course, it was." He pushed back his chair, then stood. He leaned down, resting his hand on Ethan's shoulder as he pressed a kiss to the top of Ethan's head. He smoothed his thumb over the material of Ethan's jacket, his hand lingering as he maintained a connection.

"Everything okay?" Ethan glanced up at him with bright, curious eyes.

A ticklish sensation spread through his chest. He smiled as he met Ethan's eyes. "Yeah." He pulled back his hand. "I'll be right back."

He scratched at the flutter over his heart with his thumb. What was that about?

"We're hoping for a Hawaii wedding," Dolly said with a bright smile. She hugged the arm of the man beside her —Simon—who it turned out had shared home room with Ethan. Felix suppressed a smirk when Ethan nodded, his lips pressed together in a pout as he stared between Dolly and her fiancé. It seemed he was no closer to remembering who Simon was.

"Sounds lovely," said one of the men in the group that Felix and Ethan had found themselves standing with.

Zed, Felix remembered. He had a name that stood out. Felix glanced down when Ethan took his hand and was frowning at Zed who appeared to be smirking back.

Was Ethan okay?

Felix squeezed Ethan's hand by way of encouragement. When they had joined the group, the conversation had been Simon reminiscing about being on the school football team. It seemed some of the others had also been on the team, including Zed.

Maybe I should find us an escape route. Dolly had, for

some reason, taken it upon herself to talk to Ethan, encouraging him out of his seat and half-dragging him by the wrist to join the group. Was she overcompensating for something? Maybe she had been like this in high school, one of those people eager, or maybe instructed by teachers, to bring the quiet kids into the fold and get them to take part.

Her intentions seemed to be genuine. *I'm probably worried over nothing.*

Talk had switched from football to further education and career paths, which Ethan had handled fine, then to Dolly's upcoming wedding.

"How about you, Ethan? Think you'll ever get married?" the man next to Zed asked. "You can do that sort of thing these days, right?"

Ethan looked at the man opposite him. Felix couldn't recall his name even though he had heard it just moments before. Ethan shifted his feet as if he were about to say something, but he remained silent, instead tightening his hold on Felix's hand. When Felix considered stepping in, it was Dolly who spoke up. "Of course, he can. Where have you been? Under a rock?" Felix was surprised by the sass in her voice, also grateful as Ethan's grip lessened.

"He was just asking," Simon said and hugged her shoulder. "Things change all the time, don't they?"

Dolly tensed her jaw but nodded.

The group fell into silence.

That had killed the mood. Felix glanced over his shoulder. There were a few people on the dance floor now. He tugged on Ethan's arm until Ethan faced him.

He leaned in close to Ethan's ear and asked, "Want to dance?"

Ethan side-eyed the man who had spoken out. "Sure." He stared up at Felix.

Felix smiled wide, the fluttering in his chest making small ripples of warmth fan out through him.

What was this sudden urge to want to protect him?

He nodded, then scanned the group of people they had been conversing with. "Sorry to steal Ethan away, but I want to dance with my boyfriend," he said so everyone could hear him above the music. "It was lovely meeting you all." He didn't hesitate to lead Ethan by the hand, escaping the uncomfortable situation they had ended up in.

He walked with Ethan to the small dance floor, not caring to look back. It didn't matter whether they were high school students or grown adults, people could still be ignorant assholes.

They stopped on the far side of the room. The song playing was something Felix recognized but couldn't name. A middle-of-the-road kind of pace to the melody. He kept hold of Ethan's hand, swaying it as he tried to channel the feeling of being drunk, the kind of drunk where somebody thought they had the dancing prowess of Travolta.

This was a terrible idea. He watched Ethan. *Or maybe it wasn't.*

If nothing else, Ethan was smiling again as he shuffled from one foot to the other. He stared down at his feet as if calculating his footing.

"You seem distracted," Felix began with care. "Is everything okay?"

Ethan didn't launch into one of his monologues. If anything, he was silent for way longer than Felix expected him to be. Then he sighed. "Just having trouble remembering everyone. I don't think I really joined in much at school. Too much time studying, I guess. If I could go back and do it all again…"

Felix didn't press for more information, instead he decided in that moment that he needed to be a distraction so Ethan could have time to think.

"So, is there a science to dancing, too?" He moved closer so Ethan could hear him.

Ethan shook his head. "I don't think so. Or at least, not a field of science I know. I could look into it."

Felix laughed. "Please don't." He raised his and Ethan's hand, encouraged him to spin under his arm and into a hug.

"Sorry," Ethan said when he stepped on Felix's foot.

Felix squeezed him, then leaned back so he could look into Ethan's eyes. He held Ethan by the waist as they swayed, making steps back and forth. Ethan was warm where their bodies pressed together, and Felix found himself lost in the shine of Ethan's eyes beneath the lights of the dance floor.

They stayed that way for a short while, each staring into the other's eyes, until Ethan turned his face and gently pushed at Felix's chest.

"I… erm… I'm going to go find the restrooms." He straightened his jacket by the collar. "Would you mind getting me another drink? Just a soda or something?"

"Not a problem." They left the floor together but didn't separate straight away. "Is everything okay?" he asked when Ethan seemed to hesitate.

Ethan breathed in, glancing across the room, then back to Felix. "Thanks," he said.

"For what?"

"Just thanks." Ethan shrugged. "For dancing with me. Or whatever." He was cute when he was flustered.

"Sure," Felix said. "Just a soda, yes?" He thumbed toward the bar.

"Please. I'll meet you back here." Ethan rubbed Felix's shoulder, slid his hand down Felix's arm until he brushed the back of Felix's hand. "Thanks." He headed out of the room and into the corridor.

Felix ordered two sodas, then stood in view of the exit before placing the drinks on a nearby table and folding his arms across his chest. He scanned the room, noting the remnants of the group they had been with earlier. Dolly was there with Simon, along with what seemed to be another couple. Zed and the bulky man, as well as some of the others, seemed to have split off from the rest once he and Ethan had removed themselves from any further conversation.

Felix twisted his arm, checked his watch. He had no idea how long it had been since Ethan went to use the restroom. It probably was nowhere near as long as it felt.

A minute, an hour, a whole day. He sucked on his teeth as he stared at the people on the dance floor and watched the patterns of colorful lights dance across them.

What was the uneasiness he felt in his chest? It was

ridiculous. He was just here to play a role. A fake. And yet, he didn't like that Ethan was out of his sight.

I want to go find him.

Felix decided to do just that, left the room, and followed signs to the bathroom. He entered, rounded a corner, and was shocked and worried to find Ethan standing with his back to him, crowded by three men. He eyed the one in the middle and flexed his fingers. He didn't know what the hell was going on here, but he was ready to jump in.

"Ethan?" he said and stepped closer.

Ethan looked over his shoulder. He was pale, his expression grim.

What the hell was going on?

Chapter Six

Ethan had gotten to the point where he was either going to climb Felix like a tree or do something embarrassing, like kiss him in the middle of the dance floor. He was losing himself in the romantic narrative of what tonight was supposed to be and needed to remember this wasn't some *Cinderella* tale where he got his prince in the end— this was a booking he'd paid for. It was just that Felix was so attentive and thoughtful, and seemed to know exactly what to do to make Ethan's life easier. He used dancing to get them away from the wedding conversation, made cocktails to keep Ethan's nerves at bay, and in all things, was the perfect date. Five stars, would recommend.

I'm attracted to this version of Felix.

Not that this was news to Ethan—he'd been attracted to the image of Felix for a long time, seeing him in photos through Jared, and not that often at all. He'd mostly kept Felix at a distance, but there was something happening tonight that was different—

because Felix made Ethan feel cared for, desirable and desired.

Which was why Ethan needed some space right now before he did something stupid and forgot about the contract. He hurried down the corridor, following the signs for the bathrooms, and shoved the outer door open so fast that he almost hit somebody coming the other way. He and his almost-victim did a weird, awkward dance where the other guy looked down at Ethan's badge, and then, back up to his face with an accompanying blank expression, all while Ethan glanced at the man's badge, and did the same.

"Sorry," Ethan said.

"No worries." The man he'd walked into sidestepped, and this time Ethan went the opposite way with his own soft apology. The cohort for that year in school had been over a hundred, large for the exclusive private school, so there was no way Ethan was going to remember everyone. Right?

Take the weird guy who'd been hovering on the edge of the wedding conversation earlier. The one who had made Ethan's skin prickle with some kind of recognition just out of his reach.

Dressed in a blue suit that was two sizes too big, the man was tall and wide, and carried an air of disappointment around him, as if he felt the world had done him wrong. He gave off vibes that he didn't want to be here, yet he seemed to hang around every group of people Ethan had been talking to. Ethan didn't recognize him, and his name badge was hidden under a suit jacket, but the man kept staring at him, and it unsettled Ethan. He'd tried to picture him younger, maybe with more hair, slimmer, but still, nothing was coming to mind about who he might be. He was also not talking to Ethan, hadn't introduced himself, and Ethan got the feeling he was deliberately hiding his badge.

All kinds of weird.

The bathroom was empty. He rested his hands on the counter and stared at his reflection, giving himself a chance to work through all the thoughts that jumbled in his head and made no sense. For a second, he observed himself in the mirror—as Jared often said, he scrubbed up well, his blond hair was neat for a change, he hadn't spilled anything down his suit, and he felt he wasn't out of place at this fancy event. A couple of people had come up to him, complimented him on how he was dressed and said hello. Some of them even had memories of things that connected them to him, and they relayed them with a certain fondness that confused him.

I remember you from Chem; you were my partner for a whole week; it's the only time I got an A.

Remember that time we had to do that speech, and you spoke so fast and for so long that I didn't have to say anything?

Weren't you on the chess team? You were good.

Too many observations, too few memories he could recall, add in the unfortunate attraction to Felix, and Ethan needed some space. It didn't help that his head was spinning a little from the cocktail and the initial whiskey, and that was probably what was giving him all the strange thoughts about what he'd like to do with Felix.

He was halfway through washing his hands when the door opened. Ethan glanced up and caught the new arrival in the mirror, the disappointed man in the ill-fitting suit.

"Hi, Ethan."

Ethan glanced at where the guy's badge should be, but it was still hidden. Great, there went his chance of being able to fudge his way through this.

"I'm sorry, I don't…" He turned off the tap and shook his fingers before crossing to the tidy pile of small hand towels, wiping his hands, and depositing the used towel in a wicker basket. "It's been quite the evening, and I'm not remembering everybody as well as I'd like."

"Marcus. Uhmm… Football." Marcus seemed nervous—didn't know quite where to look.

A twinge of fear settled in Ethan's chest, but he put that down to the fact he now had to find conversation, and that was a very real fear in itself. *Marcus, football.* Ethan had never had much to do with the football team way back when, happier playing chess or working through lunch hours on science projects. The school as a whole had been behind the Warriors football team, but what Ethan *could* recall was they'd been shit. Still, as in most schools, the sports stars, failing or not, had been royalty, the same as cheerleaders. He didn't remember a single thing about his interaction with either of those groups.

The door opened again; this time two more men joined them. Marcus blanched—shooting a glance at

Ethan, and then seemed to change before his eyes. From cautious and worried, he blustered and pushed his shoulders back. What the fuck was happening here? Ethan expected the new arrivals to walk past, but instead they joined Marcus in staring at him.

This is weird. I don't like it.

"Nice to meet you. Now, if you'll excuse me, my boyfriend—"

"Stay!" one of the new arrivals said. "My man Marcus here has some things he wants to say to you." Zed was all shiny suit and a loudmouth who made a big show of telling everybody how successful his insurance company was. Ethan guessed that was part of what reunions were about—proving to people you'd made something of your life after you left school. He hadn't even bothered explaining in full about what he was doing for a career, summing it up in one word—science —and nobody had seemed that surprised.

Ethan was gripped with an uneasy feeling at the way Marcus had changed in front of him. Also, Zed hadn't moved from the door, and the other man with him— Johnny, according to his badge, had a smile that could be called feral.

Marcus. Zed. Johnny.

Football.

I don't feel so good.

"You weren't at the five-year reunion?" Zed raised a single eyebrow. Age hadn't been kind to him, he was soft around the edges, but he was tall and broad, and Ethan had the feeling he was used to muscling into things. He had a way of holding himself that was having a strange effect on Ethan. There was hurt, fear, shame—it began in his belly, and curved and cut its way up to his chest.

"Probably scared that Marcus would knock him to the ground," Johnny said, then snorted a laugh.

What? Why would Marcus want to do that? *Okay, I need to defuse whatever is going on here.*

"I didn't think anyone actually went to five-year reunions?" Ethan joked, and underscored the words with his practiced smile, the one Jared told him he needed to use if he didn't feel confident.

"Well, we were all there, waiting to talk to you about what you did to Marcus," Johnny said, and took a step closer to stand at Marcus's side. Zed stayed where he was, and there was something about this feeling of being trapped that was familiar to Ethan.

"Talk to me about what?"

"Talking *at* you, more like," Zed said.

"I was probably too busy to go," Ethan said after a pause.

Zed snorted a laugh. "Busy, eh? Hear that, Johnny? Science-boy was busy."

"Probably saving dolphins." Johnny smirked.

"Dolphins would be cetology. I focus mainly on chemistry, through the use of…" Ethan stopped talking when words failed him.

Dolphins. Science-boy. Marcus. Football.

Marcus took a step closer, now within reach of Ethan, who had edged back until his ass hit the counter. His expression was cautious, his posture wrong—as if he was forcing himself into character. None of this made sense. Ethan didn't have anywhere else to go, and unless someone else came into the bathroom, it was just him and three others who unsettled him to the point where he felt like he might crumble. Was this one of the open doors? Was it something he'd buried, or maybe hadn't even realized was happening to him? Were Marcus, Zed, and Johnny bullies in adult life? Did that imply they'd been bullies at school, football kings who smashed and trod their way through sensitive kids, or the ones who liked science, or dancing—anyone they could torment to make themselves feel as though they had control over everything.

I don't have control.

"Do it, Marcus," Zed encouraged. "Show him it's not right what he did to you."

"What did I do to you? I'm sorry, I don't recall—"

Marcus placed a hand on the counter and leaned in. Ethan had nowhere to move to and panic gripped him as a memory began to coalesce. At first, it was nothing but smoke, but then he began to identify noise in the memory, music, and the bright twinkling lights of the prom, him in the washroom, gathering the courage to mingle like Julian suggested he should.

Marcus had been there—in the bathroom with him. He'd cornered Ethan, and a sense memory of him kissing, his hands gripping Ethan's hips, cupping him, feeling him, flooded back one visceral moment at a time.

"I need to leave," Ethan managed. "Leave alone."

Marcus reached for him, and Ethan felt nauseated. No longer was he a grown man with a career, working on his confidence, hoping one day for romance with a partner who loved him for who he was… Right here in this bathroom he was just the senior who'd been looking for acceptance, and who'd somehow found himself on the radar of one of the football team members.

"What's up, little Ethan? Marcus isn't touching you," Zed sneered. "My boy here wants to clear up some misconceptions after what you did to him—"

"What? When Marcus pushed me back against this basin and—"

Johnny snorted. "See, that's where you got your story wrong, the queer kid came onto to the footballer, assaulted Marcus. I saw everything."

There was no sense in that statement, none at all. Not only was Marcus an entire head taller than Ethan, but he was also twice as broad, and Ethan had been kinda skinny back in school. Skinny and small. He couldn't force a kiss on Marcus even if that was the kind of thing he did.

Which it wasn't.

"No one was in the bathroom, no one saw!" Ethan snapped, as memories coalesced. "That's why…" Ethan's world shifted as the horror of feeling trapped that night spilled over. That was his open door? A memory he'd hidden from himself. He didn't remember much from the prom; he'd drunk so much that he'd blanked it all out. He just remembered Julian asking him if he was okay.

"I saw what you did to Marcus," Johnny said. "I walked in and saw your hands all over him, watched you paw him before running off. He didn't have to tell us anything when I could see what you did."

"What?" Ethan shoved at Marcus who stumbled back. "No."

The bathroom door opened again, but this time it was Felix who stepped inside, and all Ethan could feel was a familiar embarrassment and shame that someone would see what was happening, and that this someone was Felix. His date bypassed Zed and was, suddenly, in the middle of everything. There was complete silence as Felix stepped between Marcus and Ethan.

"Hi, guys," he said with veiled warning, but Ethan didn't need to be rescued right now. The memory that had escaped from where he'd hidden it was so clear he shook with emotion.

"Marcus tried to kiss me at prom." Ethan gripped Felix's arm. "He pushed me against the counter... I didn't even know him. Stayed away from him. Everyone hated the football team."

Marcus went pale—wouldn't meet Ethan's gaze, as everything fell out of him in a panic, but it was tinged with frustrated anger, and he felt Felix tense under his hold. His feet apart, his stance loose, Felix seemed as if he was going to fight for Ethan in that moment.

"Okay," Felix said, as if Ethan hadn't just told him the worst of things. "Who do I need to kill first?" He sounded so focused, but Ethan knew he had to do this himself.

"I need to close my own door," Ethan insisted.

After a moment where they exchanged pointed glances—Felix questioning, and Ethan answering he was okay—Felix stepped to one side, but he didn't go far. The fact Felix had listened to the unspoken plea for

Ethan to be left to handle things on his own was a revelation, but he couldn't focus on that right now.

Zed didn't appear quite as confident now that Felix was here, if anything, he appeared more than a little fearful. Typical bully, only good when they had the upper hand. Johnny seemed confused, and Marcus was quiet. Ethan glanced at him. He was pale, and he seemed... scared.

It was Johnny who broke the impasse. "Hang on, Marcus; Zed told me that it was Ethan who tried it on with you," Johnny said. "When Zed came in and he had his hands on you, was it because it was actually you...?" It appeared he couldn't find the words to explain what he meant.

He should try living with it like I had. Or hadn't as the case may be, given how far Ethan had buried the memory.

"He's a lying piece of shit," Marcus snapped—all the vulnerability sliding away. "I ain't no fucking homo."

"But, you know, science-boy's always been kinda small," Johnny mused, "and you've always been kinda big. I'm not getting this," he muttered. "What's going on?"

"I'm closing my damn door!" Ethan snapped.

They all stared at him in confusion. Then he gripped Felix by the hand, tilted his chin, and forced his way past all three men.

Johnny attempted to stop Ethan leaving. "Hey, Ethan, look, I'm sorry if—"

"Fuck off," Ethan snapped, and tugged Felix out of the bathroom and into the hallway. Without stopping, he went through the room with Felix in tow, passing tables of people chatting as though they hadn't a care in the world, then registration where Ethan unpinned his badge and dropped it onto the desk, headed through the double doors, and into the cold beyond.

"Wait," Felix said, turned back, and within seconds returned with their coats. He handed Ethan his, but all Ethan could do was stand in shock as snowflakes whirled around his head.

"I'm so angry!" Ethan forced out; his words staccato sharp. "I didn't want him to kiss me. I didn't expect anyone to kiss me at prom, but if it was going to be my first kiss, I wanted it to mean something. It meant nothing, apart from me having ten years of not understanding why I am the way I am. I chase people away as soon as they get close, I fall for the wrong guys, and I never understand what I'm doing or why I am doing it. Do you know how many people have just run the other way because I've been awkward as shit as soon as they tried to kiss me?" He was shaking now, and he could feel tears pricking his eyes—angry, frustrated tears.

Felix zipped up Ethan's thick downy coat, buttoning it to the chin and making sure the hood was up and covering his hair. Ethan was already shivering, but he wasn't sure if that was because of the metaphorical door he'd stepped through, or because of the actual door leading to the real cold outside.

"I want to go back and beat him into a bloody pulp." Felix bristled with anger, forcing his hands into his pockets.

"That won't help anything."

"I know, but I want to." He stopped for a moment, as if he needed to get control of his emotions. "Do you want to call someone? Jared? The cops?"

"Jared has enough to worry about, and no to the cops. I don't know what I want to do. Can you just let me think on what needs to happen next?"

"Of course, but if he did it then, it could be that he's still out there…"

"Yeah, I get that. But my memories are messed up, and what if I'm wrong?"

They stood in silence for a moment, the snow growing heavier, huddled close to each other on the edge of a puddle of brightness thrown by a security light.

"I'm sorry your prom was ruined," Felix offered.

Ethan sighed. "I don't know much about it to be fair; I got drunk. Anyway, you don't need to feel sorry for me. I mean, I wasn't lonely you know, I had my science. Only it's not science that makes you want the fairytale that is your first kiss at prom."

Ethan's voice was scratchy, and he leaned into Felix as his date gathered him into his arms and held him tight.

His heart hurt, because even as he'd tried to close the door, it was almost impossible to face what had happened tonight. He'd wanted a kiss—a perfect kiss on a perfect night. Was that too much to ask?

"Let me," Felix murmured.

"What?"

"Will you let me try and give you the perfect kiss,

pretend it's prom, right here in the snow?" Felix tilted Ethan's chin, then cradled his face, his hands cold and his eyes filled with emotion. Felix was so beautiful, his smile so genuine, the compassion in his gaze so deep that Ethan lost himself in their depths.

For a moment he considered saying no, wanted to joke that his contract didn't cover perfect kisses in the snow, maybe add that he didn't need rescuing, and that he wanted to make it all end.

But then, Felix leaned in.

And it felt so right.

Ethan sighed into the kiss, which was so unlike any kiss he'd ever felt before. He didn't know what was different, but Felix cradled his face, held him as if he was a delicate thing, and then deepened the kiss. Ethan wasn't panicking, there was no desperate need to yank himself away, if anything he wanted to stay here in this moment, forever. Felix was strong, and gentle, and the way their tongues tangled, and the taste of Felix… it was so much, and so perfect.

When they separated, Ethan kept his eyes shut, a whisper of snowflakes on his heated skin. "Wow," was all he could manage.

"Was that okay?" Felix pulled Ethan into a hug. "I guess… Happy belated Prom?"

Ethan wanted to hug him back, but this wasn't real. He eased himself away from Felix before he did something stupid and asked for another kiss.

"Thank you."

"Can we talk?" For a moment Ethan thought this

was Felix talking to him, but then he realized the voice was coming from behind them. Marcus.

He'd followed them outside, without a coat, shivering and hugging his middle, looking as if he was about to cry.

"No," Ethan said before he could rethink everything. He wanted tonight to end with a kiss, not fear of something in his past. "Felix, please?"

Felix bundled him into the car, and Ethan refused to meet Marcus's gaze. It was only when they were on the road that Ethan could breathe again.

"Are you okay?" Felix squeezed his knee.

"Yeah," Ethan lied. "Awesome."

"If you want to talk about—"

"Thank you for tonight, for being my date. You were very… professional."

He thought he saw Felix wince but couldn't be sure. Great. Now he'd insulted the owner of the lips that had given him the best kiss of his life.

"Would you give me ten out of ten?" Felix smiled after a pause.

"After that kiss?" Ethan murmured. "At least a six."

Felix pressed a hand to his chest as if he'd been wounded, but at least they were back to normal, and the weirdness of the kiss, the all-consuming heat of it, could be filed away to think about later.

Chapter Seven

Snow. Ethan. Kiss.

Felix brushed his finger over his lips. It had been three days, and his head was still at that damn school reunion. He had texted Ethan a couple of times to check up on him and make sure he was okay. He felt for Ethan but wasn't sure he should get too involved.

I was just hired to play a role.

He had decided it was better to let Jared deal with his friend and any aftermath.

I should contact him again, or maybe Jared. Just to put my mind at ease.

"Felix. Hey, Felix."

Felix raised his eyes and stared at Rowan, who was sitting opposite him. "Sorry, what?"

With a sigh, Rowan said, "I asked if you have any questions about tomorrow?" He pressed his palms to his desk, resting them either side of the paperwork they had been discussing.

"Tomorrow?"

"The Lomas Shelter fundraiser. The job you're working with Caleb," said Rowan.

The run-up to the holiday season was always hectic, but somehow it seemed more so than usual this year. *Well, I did say I'd take anything, as long as it was over and done the same day.* "Right, the fundraiser."

"Caleb is going to be arriving late, so you need to cover the… Felix?"

"I'm listening, Caleb is going to be late, so I need to cover the… cover what?"

"Caleb will message you when he's ten minutes out, and you need to… are you even listening to me?" Rowan quirked an eyebrow. He leaned across the desk and snapped his fingers in front of Felix's face. "Focus, Felix."

"I am."

I am not. The day was dragging as if it might never end. He was tired and distracted and wanted to go home.

Leaning forward, Rowan sniffed. "Have you been drinking?"

"What?" Felix sat back. "No. Of course not." He paused. "Oh. Actually, I did have a couple of glasses of wine." He had been on a job through lunch and into the afternoon. There had been an orchestra, a buffet— which had the tiniest gourmet hamburgers he had ever seen—and free wine. All very fancy.

"Only a couple?"

What was Rowan implying? "Yes, a couple. It was paid for so…"

Rowan narrowed his eyes.

"I was just following the client's lead. I'm not drunk, if that's what you're getting at."

"Did I say that?" Rowan leaned back in his chair. "Is something worrying you? Did something happen earlier? Everything was signed off ready to be filed, so I assumed it went well. You've not pulled a Jared have you? You didn't touch a T-Rex's toe, and the whole thing collapsed or something?"

Poor Jared, always in trouble for something, even when he wasn't present.

Felix laughed. "No. I kept my hands firmly in my pockets." His date had been to a private function held at a museum. He hadn't needed or been given the specifics but was aware the party was for someone who had made a large monetary donation to the restoration of one of the exhibition wings.

He met Rowan's eyes. Doubt was etched on Rowan's brow. Felix insisted, "Everything is fine. Honestly. My mind wandered, is all."

"Hmm." Rowan squinted. "Are you worried about working with Caleb? I know he's new here and has a reputation for being a workaholic, but he's good at his job, and he can switch from one to another fast."

"No, I like Caleb, he's... yeah. It's not him."

"Okay, so how're your parents? Everything okay there?"

Felix nodded. He appreciated Rowan being concerned about him. "They're well. Thank you." He cleared his throat. "It's probably the time of year. Dark and cold and busy. Or, maybe, they were bigger glasses of wine than I thought." He chuckled softly. "Sorry."

"Okay. If you're sure." Rowan shuffled the papers in front of him. "So, do you have any questions?"

"I don't—" He raised his hip when his cell phone vibrated and smiled awkwardly at Rowan because of the interruption. Guilt crept through him as he pulled out his phone, but he couldn't ignore it. What if it was his parents? He checked. It wasn't his parents, but someone else who seemed to be taking up a lot of real estate in his thoughts: Ethan.

"Do you need to answer that?"

Felix considered what to do. Ethan would have to wait. He ignored the call and rested it screen-down on his leg. "Sorry about that. I'll call them back. Where were we? Oh, right, no I don't have any questions. At least, I can't think of anything."

"Okay. The car will pick you up at two, go onto to the client's home, then to the venue." Rowan slid the sheet containing the day's itinerary across the desk and tapped the corner of the page. "A copy of the main points to take away with you. If you do think of anything, you know you can call or message me at any time."

"Any time?"

Rowan huffed a breath. "Within reason, obviously."

"I know. And thanks." He took the paper, glancing at it before folding it in half. The job for tomorrow was straightforward. His role was to link arms with the client and look pretty at their side. He was just there to be shown off.

"Is that everything?" he asked.

Rowan tidied the remaining papers into a pile. "For

now. We'll discuss your current block of bookings in our next meeting." He opened his diary and flipped between pages. "That will be on Wednesday."

"I remember—" Felix clicked his tongue when his cell vibrated. He turned over his phone. Ethan? He ignored the call again. He felt bad, but he wanted to finish the meeting properly. He'd been distracted; he couldn't deny that.

I should at least end on a professional note. I'll call him back as soon as I get out of here.

"I'm really sorry," he uttered.

Rowan smiled. "We're done anyway." He picked up the paperwork, tapped them so they lined up. "Good luck tomorrow."

"Thanks." He stood, wincing as his cell vibrated and Ethan's name popped up on the screen. "I should get this."

Rowan waved him away.

When he was out of earshot, Felix answered the call. "Hello."

Ethan blurted, "Finally."

"I was in a meeting."

"I know; Jared said."

"Then why— You know what, whatever." He made his way downstairs. "So, what's up?"

"It's an emergency. You have to help me." Ethan spoke quickly, a slight whine in his tone.

"Help you? Has something happened?" His thoughts went back to the school reunion and the scene he had walked in on in the restroom. "You're okay, right?"

"No. I'm not. It's terrible. He tagged me, and they saw them."

Felix stopped as he reached the building's main door. He struggled to fasten his coat with one hand and tilted his head to one side, staring through an advertisement poster on the wall as he tried to figure out what Ethan was talking about. "Tagged?"

"Yes. And it's too late to undo it. They saw them already."

"Huh?" Felix was starting to think maybe he was drunk after all. Ethan wasn't making sense. He opened the door and left the building. "Ethan, you're going to have to use all your words today because I have no idea what you are talking about."

He made his way down the steps to the sidewalk. "Ethan?" He waited. "Are you still there?"

"Felix." Ethan's voice echoed in stereo.

Felix looked over his shoulder when someone gripped his arm.

"Help." Ethan appeared beside him.

Felix lowered his phone. He didn't know what to say. Ethan was right there, his blue eyes wide and desperate, and his cheeks puffed out, and flushed from the cold. "What are you doing here?" Felix gave a quick shake of his head, regaining his focus. "How did you know I was here?"

"I already told you. I asked Jared. He said you had a meeting, so I came here."

"Oh yeah." He pulled Ethan to one side. "That still doesn't answer my question. Why are you here? Is this to do with that Marcus guy at the reunion?" Felix peered past Ethan as if he expected Marcus to be right there, and he flinched when he realized his hands were curled into fists. Violence was not the answer, but the kiss in the snow, and the fear Ethan had been feeling, were both moments that had permanent residence in Felix's brain.

Ethan huffed. "As I said. Julian tagged me in his silly photos, and now, everyone wants to meet my boyfriend."

No, you didn't say that at all.

"Okay." Felix had a slight handle on what was going on. "So, you've been tagged on social media by Julian in the photos he was taking at the reunion, yes?"

"Yes."

"And I'm there, too, labeled or assumed to be your boyfriend?"

"Yes. That's what I said."

Felix looked at Ethan. *You really didn't.* He took a deep breath. "So?"

"You need to be my boyfriend again." Ethan grabbed him and held him tightly. "Please."

"—and then, suddenly, they all started talking to me about things that weren't work or to do with the lab. It was so weird and kind of scary. They stood so close, and everybody was looking at me."

Felix leaned his head in his hand and listened to Ethan's rant. They had taken their discussion indoors, ending up in Rhea's, the bar Jared's boyfriend, Nate, owned.

"I don't even remember accepting friend requests from any of them. But now they all think you're my boyfriend and want to meet you." He waved his hands around. "What do I do?"

"You could tell them I was just a friend you invited to tag along."

Ethan chewed on his lip. "I already confirmed you were my boyfriend. I just wanted them to leave me alone. I had work I needed to do. My paper's not going to write itself. But then Carol said I should bring you to the department's Christmas party."

"And what did you say?"

"I was so flustered by people talking to me, I might have agreed to go and that I would bring you with me."

Felix scratched the back of his head. "Fine. Then tell them you asked, but I'm busy. Say I'm out of town because of work or something on that day."

"Plus, Jenny's engagement party in the New Year."

"That day, too."

"And the celebratory drinks because Daniel got published in a journal."

Seriously?

Felix clenched his teeth. "Then how about, I'm out of town for the rest of the month. January as well." He eyed Ethan. "All year?" Ethan diverted his eyes. "Then, should we go with I've moved across the country, you didn't want a long-distance relationship, so we split up?"

"Doesn't that seem a bit farfetched?"

Felix sat back. "Then, what do *you* want to do?" He was pretty sure he knew the answer and was ready to curse Jared and his *favor*.

"Could you please pretend to be my boyfriend for a little longer?" Ethan clasped his hands together as he begged, "At least for the Christmas dinner, as that's really soon. I'll figure something out for the others, promise." He reached across the table and took hold of Felix's hand. "I'll hire you like last time. Keep it all proper and through Rowan and stuff as long as it isn't too expensive. Not that I want you to do it for free, but money..." He paused, and then smiled. "Please." His eyes were bright, his expression hopeful.

Felix glanced at Ethan's hand on his. The same light and fluttery feeling from the school reunion, and on any time he remembered the moments they had shared through the night, rose in his chest.

"Okay," he finally said. "I'll do it."

Ethan's expression softened, his shoulders dropping in relief. "Thank you."

Felix nodded. "Sure."

After all, what could go wrong?

Chapter Eight

Ethan was good at solving problems, in fact he was great at them. After all, what was chemistry, but one giant puzzle. All it took was writing down the variables, looking for catalysts, and checking results. So why wasn't this working? He eyed the board with Marcus's name at the top and added a couple more pink Post-it notes to the right of the yellow ones. Pink was for questions, yellow was facts, but there was a lot more pink on this board than he wanted at this stage. The cold, hard fact was that a kiss in the bathroom with Marcus had happened at the prom, and he knew he hadn't wanted it. He knew Marcus's name, where he lived—given he'd inherited his parents' house when they'd retired to Florida—and that he wasn't married. Nor did he have kids, or much in the way of extended family, and he was partner in a garage. That much Ethan had found out online. He had added each tiny detail in the correct place, and yet, still none of it was making sense.

"What are you up to?" Jared asked from behind

him. Ethan jumped a foot and slammed his closet door shut before his friend could see what he was doing. He still hadn't told Jared the full details of what had happened at the reunion, even though he knew he should, if only to get everything off his chest. He'd confirmed to Jared that he'd closed a metaphorical door, and then nodded when Jared had asked if he was okay. Spoiler—he wasn't okay. All the memories surrounding Marcus were messing with his head. Add in his unfortunately timed and mind-blowing attraction to Felix, plus his growing pile of research and writing, and he was all over the place.

"Ethan?" Jared prompted.

"Nothing's wrong," Ethan blurted, which wasn't an exact answer to the question he'd been asked.

Jared stared at him, and Ethan was convinced that Jared knew something was going on.

"I don't know what to do," he admitted. "It's all messed up in my head."

Jared continued to stare at him for a moment, and then reached past him for the closet door, his hand hovering near the handle. He waited, asking silently for Ethan's permission to look at what was in there. Ashamed and lost, Ethan nodded. Jared pulled out the pin board with its neat Post-it notes. It was all Ethan could do to stand, and in the end, he sat on his bed and crossed his legs.

Jared examined the two boards. "Marcus? Who's that?"

Ethan wasn't sure where to start, but Jared was the one person who might be able to steer him through this so he could shut that stupid door from school. He'd already received an email from Johnny explaining that he hadn't known what happened, that all his information had been secondhand from Zed, but the message had been long and detailed. In it, he admitted he'd denied to himself all the evidence pointing to the fact his best friend from school was an asshole. Ethan wanted to reply, to tell him everything was okay, to exonerate Johnny for not understanding the situation, even suggesting it wasn't his fault. But the logical part of him understood that Marcus, plus both of his friends, were all integral to the mess in his head, and that forgiveness shouldn't be so easily doled out. Hence, the pin board.

"There's another one in there, behind the coat." Ethan pointed at the closet.

Jared rummaged around and pulled out a second pin board. This one had orange and green Post-it notes, and just the title alone made Ethan squirm in embarrassment.

"The Ethan-Felix hypothesis," Jared read, and glanced at him in confusion.

"See?" Ethan could hear how miserable he sounded. "I have two problems, and I don't know where to start with either of them."

Jared nodded. "Okay, do you want to talk about it? Or do you want me to try to make sense of everything? Do I need to get coffee for us both? Or do you want to throw these things back in the closet and sit in front of Nat Geo?"

Ethan's heart swelled, and he loved that Jared knew

which options Ethan might choose right now. But, as much as he wanted to sit on the sofa and binge watch the newest episode of *Gold Rush*, he needed answers more.

"I can't work with any of this," Ethan muttered, "my brain." He knew it didn't make much sense just saying that, but he tapped his head anyway.

Jared nodded as if he understood. "Okay then, start from the beginning. Who is this Marcus? Given these are photos from the yearbook, I assume that this Marcus guy was your classmate in high school?"

"He was an open door," Ethan admitted.

Jared's eyes widened. "Go on."

"He was something I'd blanked out, but when I went to the reunion, everything that'd happened with him flooded back. I was in the bathroom, all dressed up for prom, and I had the biggest crush on this boy, Anthony, but Marcus came into the bathroom. It just flooded back that he'd kissed me at prom, but I don't remember it being a nice kiss. It was him trying to take something from me that I didn't want to give him, and that is a big reason why I would have forgotten it or blanked it out."

"Did he hurt you?" Jared asked with a fierceness that Ethan appreciated.

He kind of needed someone in his corner right now, and it felt good when Jared sat next to him on the bed, placing his arm over Ethan's shoulders.

"I don't remember everything. Maybe being scared? I don't know. But yeah, he was on the football team and was a lot bigger than me, he still is, and I imagine that if I hadn't got away, maybe—"

"I'll kill him," Jared interrupted, and his furious reaction made Ethan wince.

"No, you won't," Ethan began to explain, having in his head all the reasons why it wasn't a good idea for Jared to go to prison. "I don't recall everything that happened, and you being convicted of a crime, would—"

"Okay then, maybe I can accidentally maim him."

"Still prison," Ethan reminded him.

Jared muttered something harsh, then sighed. "What did Felix do when he found out who this guy was? Did he punch him?"

"No, he kissed me." Ethan waited for the explosion. After all, this had happened a few days ago now, and he'd fobbed off Jared's questions about the event with a generic *it was fine*. It appeared that Jared wasn't in explosion mode, though, because he settled both of the boards on the bed and sat cross-legged next to Ethan to examine them.

"Felix kissed you. This Marcus guy tried to kiss you. Ethan, for the love of all that's holy, start from the beginning."

It took them an hour just to work through the complicated reactions Ethan was having to everything going on in his life. Marcus kissing him at the prom was just confusion and memories that didn't sit right, Felix kissing him was possibly the best thing to ever happen to him. Add in the fact that Ethan had hired Felix for more work—even though his bank account would scream at him when he paid the invoices—and there was an awful lot to unpick.

Jared picked up a pen, wrote the word *police* on a green note, and added it to the Marcus board. Ethan winced that he was using the wrong note color but had to ignore it.

"That's your first stop," Jared said.

"No. Look. This happened ten years ago—I don't recall any clear details, but I do know there was a witness who has, I think, been manipulated to consider exactly what they saw. The police will likely listen to my story and then, suggest that maybe it was just some prom thing that went wrong. Or maybe they won't, and this was the only time Marcus did anything like that, and I'm throwing him under the bus."

"But Ethan—"

"And that's why I have this board because I want to fix this, and I don't want him to still be out there doing this to other people. I know that's naïve, but if I could find enough of the variables that make him who he is, then maybe I can help him shut his own metaphorical door. He's stuck in the high school loop where he used to be the big man, and I get the feeling things are slipping through his fingers in his real life now. I mean, he didn't have a partner with him, and he didn't seem to have photos of kids on his phone, he wasn't sharing anything around like the rest of them were. He didn't talk much to the other people there, certainly not about his work or what was going on in his life."

"So, I get why you don't want to go to the cops straight away." Jared huffed. "But I agree you should be worried about what he might be doing to others."

"He looked at me as if he was going to cry, Jared. I

don't think I got the whole story, and then when he followed us to the car, I told him to fuck off, and he was standing there staring at me, and he looked broken."

"Guilt?"

"Maybe, or secrets, or… I don't know."

"Then, first stop, is to think more about the Marcus thing. Maybe talk to the guy?" Jared side-hugged him. "And then, we move on to the kiss with Felix."

Ethan groaned and twisted his hands in his hair. "I don't even know…"

"Well, to summarize about the kiss," Jared began, after he stared at the boards for a few more minutes. "I think you're looking at this hypothesis in completely the wrong way."

"But it's science—"

"It's not science; it's magic," Jared announced as if that made complete sense.

"Magic isn't real—"

"Shh. You shouldn't have two separate boards right now, you realize that?" He forged ahead without waiting for an answer. "What happened with Marcus didn't, specifically, lead to the kiss in the parking lot, but the kiss was a reaction, like in chemistry."

Ethan's ears pricked up at that. Chemistry was something he could deal with. "Go on."

Jared tapped the board and moved a few of the Post-its around. "You plus Felix equals, I don't know, something as a base, a starting point. Then, add in cocktails, and you have your first catalyst. Then, add in having to be social, plus the Marcus incident, plus recalling what happened at school, plus—"

"This equation is getting too big," Ethan observed. He could see where this was going, and it seemed as if Jared wanted to excuse the kiss in the parking lot by detailing all the things leading up to it. Ethan wasn't sure he wanted to excuse the kiss—he'd been hoping there was an equation where the perfect kiss he and Felix had shared was just that—a kiss. He didn't want to admit that the hottest thing that ever happened to him was because of circumstances, because deep inside, he was desperate to keep the kiss as a discrete variable.

"All I'm saying is, everything that happened the rest of the night might have led to the kiss in one way or another, but that's how kisses work. They have to come from somewhere, whether it's drama, confusion, or just attraction. It's nothing more difficult to understand than the fact that you and Felix have an attraction. Like two magnets, or something." Jared made fists and knocked them together, as if he was demonstrating how magnets worked.

Ethan smiled; he loved it when Jared tried to channel science, because it was sweet that his friend took so much time trying to help him in ways Ethan understood. He was aware he could be a hard friend to have at times, but Jared didn't seem to care.

"You're saying that Felix is my magnet?" He tapped his lip.

Now it was Jared's turn to smile. "Well, he is for the time being. Have I just talked complete garbage?"

"No. I want to say Felix is a very strong magnet, but I've got myself in a situation where I've had to hire him again, or at least, I didn't *have* to hire him, but I did use some exaggerations about what my colleagues expected of me as an *excuse* to hire him. I mean, they'll soon forget if I don't bring a date to the Christmas party, or Carol's engagement, or to the celebration for Daniel getting published." Ethan frowned. "But I want to kiss Felix again, a lot, and if I hire him then, maybe, we could do some more kissing, and it might add up to more."

"Have you thought of maybe just asking him out on a date?"

Ethan rolled his eyes and pressed his thumb to his chest. "Have you seen me?"

"Cute?"

"Distracted, disorganized outside of my career. I don't really take time to think about what I'm wearing. I barely remember social details, and I have these bright flashes where I remember everything. I'm contrary. I'm an equation that doesn't balance."

"That's…" Jared huffed, and then sighed. "One day you'll actually realize you have way more to offer than you think. You're kind, and funny, and brilliant."

"Maybe then, after this Christmas event, I could ask him to come with me as my date. Only, what if he just laughs in my face? What if he says that unless he's paid—"

"You're an idiot," Jared muttered. "In the first place, you wouldn't be attracted to an asshole, and in the second place, Felix is one of the good guys."

"Okay then, I'll ask him. *After* the Christmas party."

Jared nudged my elbow. "Aww, little Ethan all grown up."

Ethan nudged him back, maybe a little hard as he tumbled off the bed, laughing like an idiot. "I hate you," he lied, but Jared couldn't hear him over the laughter.

The Christmas party was being held in the third conference room—cleared of all the whiteboards, and decorated with tinsel and lights, and a blue Christmas tree sitting in the corner. Most of the team had gone to the event straight from work, heading down the two flights of stairs from the labs. But somehow, Carol and the resident biologist, Melanie, had changed from white jackets and sensible shoes into flashy dresses and the highest heels possible. Not only that, but Carol was wearing dangling Santa earrings and had her long blonde hair tied up with a big Christmas bow. Some of the men had taken the time to change as well—Ethan noticed Daniel was looking sharp in an eggplant-colored shirt and smart pants.

As for Ethan himself? Well, he'd at least removed his lab coat and taken a few minutes in the bathroom to tidy his hair, but other than that, he was in his typical blue shirt, of which he had seven, and his dark pants, of which he had four pairs on rotation. He wasn't rocking Christmas but had pinned some holly to his shirt when Carol instructed him to. He wanted to show Felix that he *could* get into the Christmas spirit but thought maybe he needed some Dutch courage and headed straight for the table with the drinks. All year, the departments had been putting money into an account to pay for this, and there seemed to be a vast amount of alcohol, plus so many bags of chips it was impossible to count them. Later, there would be a buffet, and Carol was loud and excited that they'd managed to raise enough to get finger food catered. When faced with a vast array of alcohol, Ethan grabbed a can of soda—not quite ready to start drinking, at least not until Felix arrived.

Felix was late.

Ethan wasn't worried at first, but then, as the minutes ticked past and it was half an hour after the agreed start time for the date, he got the awful feeling that, maybe, Felix wasn't coming. Nursing his soda, he bypassed the lab techs' rendition of "Hark the Herald Angels Sing' being performed near the punchbowl and avoided the rather manic spin-the-bottle happening in the center of the room. He ended up in a quiet corner half hidden by the blue Christmas tree, hoping that with the dim lighting, he could blend in with the wall. He counted the ornaments on his side of the tree, then rearranged two of the most gaudy so that the tree was in balance, and then leaned against the wall and began to work out his exit strategy.

"… made him up. There's no way that this guy is actually dating Ethan." The words floated to Ethan past the tree, and he recognized Daniel's voice and a couple of others—Oscar and Melanie, technicians who rotated through his department.

"I bet you ten dollars this Felix guy doesn't turn up," Melanie cackled.

Ethan heard other people join in with the laughter.

"No one will take that bet; it's easy money for you," Oscar said.

From his hiding space, Ethan listened, and his embarrassment grew by the second.

"I swear there's no one that could put up with Mr. Awkward for long," Daniel said, then snorted a laugh. "He'd probably need a critical path analysis and a whiteboard hypothesis, just to get into bed with a guy."

"Oh, boyfriend, before you do that, you need to make sure that the surface is sterile." Oscar handed out his impression of Ethan to the other two laughing, and Ethan's chest tightened. *I've had sex on a non-sterile surface before.* What did they know? He eyed the exit, which was just beyond the still rowdy pass-the-parcel, and if he was stealthy enough, he could probably make it there and make his escape without anyone seeing. He didn't care what people said about him—it didn't hurt.

It hurt. He thought people liked him, or at least didn't hate him. But he didn't expect them to be laughing about him behind his back.

The main door opened, and Felix stepped inside. The noises in the room slipped away from Ethan's focus. In a sharp suit, with a glittery scarlet tie, Felix was standing still and searching the room for him. Ethan could hide, hell, he could stay behind the tree and listen to people disparage him, and laugh at him, and take bets on his sex life. Or he could take the bull by the horns, forget the Post-it notes, and do *exactly* what he wanted to do.

Determined, he stepped out from behind the tree, catching Daniel's surprised look. Then, tilting his chin in an upwards nod, he stalked to the entrance, where Felix was framed by the bright lights of the corridor beyond. He saw Felix smile, and it was the most beautiful smile he'd ever seen, and he was the most handsome man he'd ever met.

Felix held up a hand in apology. "I'm so sorry I'm late, my dad—"

Ethan cradled his face, noting the way Felix's eyes widened, and kissed him, right in front of everyone. At first, Felix was stiff, shocked, and then, boy, did he go with the flow. He rested his hands on Ethan's hips and pulled him close, then deepened the kiss, tongues tangling, the taste of him intoxicating. Ethan locked his hands behind Felix's neck and held on for dear life.

This was the perfect kiss, and it changed from a way of showing everyone the kind of person Ethan could date, to something more real.

When they separated, Felix hugged him, and whispered in his ear. "Did we do okay?" At this point, Ethan could easily fob off the kiss as pretend, but there was something in his chest, and it was tight and new, and he didn't want to lie. Ethan owed it to Felix to be honest, so that Felix had a chance to back off now, before Ethan went too far. He knew he had to be honest and tell Felix this wasn't all about fooling his work colleagues that he had a date, and that the attraction was real.

"I like you," he blurted. "More than like you. I mean. A lot. And that kiss, and all of this, it's real attraction. Okay? So, if you need to go, or you want to back off, then you can tell me." He lifted his chin. "I can take it, because I know I paid you for today and—"

Felix kissed him gently. "Shh, let's enjoy this."

Ethan wasn't sure what Felix meant by that—it wasn't exactly an answer or a firm agreement on mutual attraction, but before Felix could laugh it off, or tell him he was being stupid, or make some kind of comment about buying him, Ethan tugged his date from the doorway and into the fray.

He'd just done the scariest thing ever—been honest with Felix about him being he attracted to him and that the kiss had been more than pretend.

Now the ball was in Felix's court.

Chapter Nine

"Are you sure you don't want to swap?" Ethan shook the plastic jar of body paint. "What would I even do with this?"

Felix eyed the chocolate-flavored gift Ethan had been presented with as part of his department's secret Santa. "You think I'd want it?" He looked ahead of them as they made their way to the station. Their time at the party had passed quickly, and he was glad most of Ethan's colleagues were down-to-earth and spoke like normal human beings.

Daniel had apologized, blamed alcohol for what he'd said, but he'd been cowed by a glare from Felix when he'd heard what Daniel and the other guys had been saying. It just meant that Felix was extra attentive, and, fake or not, there'd be no doubt left in anyone's minds that he and Ethan were boyfriends.

Although, as cute as Ethan could be rattling off scientific jargon, some of what he said flew over Felix's head.

Definitely cute though.

"I guess you wouldn't."

With a chuckle, Felix took the jar from him. He unscrewed the lid. The scent of chocolate wafted from the jar, and he tapped the tip of his finger on the surface.

"What are you doing?"

"What? Were you planning on re-gifting it?"

Ethan grumbled, "Of course not. Who on earth would I give it to?" He craned his neck, eyeing the contents. "So, what exactly are you doing?"

"I was just curious." He licked his finger. It wasn't the worst chocolate he had tasted. He dipped a second finger into the spread and offered, "Wanna try?"

Ethan scrunched up his nose. "I don't think so."

"Go on." He stepped in front of Ethan. "My hands are clean. I promise."

Ethan hugged his jacket closed as they came to a stop and raised his eyebrow. "Really?" He withdrew and curled his upper lip.

"Yes. I washed them."

With a sigh, Ethan said, "Not your hands. I mean, are you sure it's edible?"

Felix twisted the jar, so the label was visible. "It says so right here." He tilted his head. "It's kind of the point." He held his hand higher.

"Hmm." Ethan shuffled closer, leaned in, and sniffed. His nose crinkled. He didn't seem convinced, but agreed, "Okay." When his lips were about to touch the top of the chocolate, Felix swiped upward, smearing the paint on Ethan's cheek. Ethan flinched back, pouting as he pawed at his face. "I should've known you'd do that."

"You should've," Felix agreed. He sucked the chocolate from his finger, smirking as he watched Ethan try to clean his cheek. "Come here." He wrapped his hand around Ethan's wrist and pulled him close. "Let me do it."

Ethan closed his eyes as Felix wiped his face. He huffed, his cheek twitching as Felix wiped with each of his fingers, removing a little at a time when he brushed Ethan's skin.

"There. All done." Felix licked his fingers.

Ethan opened his eyes. "Really?" He rubbed his cheek, then checked his palm.

"It's gone." Felix raised his hand and folded down his thumb and pinky. "I swear."

"Boy scout, my ass," Ethan said and laughed. "I can't see that at all."

Felix nodded. "You're right. I wasn't." Their eyes met for a long moment. Despite the cold weather, Felix felt warmed by Ethan's presence. Or maybe it was because of the wine he'd drunk earlier.

I don't know what to say or do.

The party had gone as expected. They had interacted and thrown out PDAs for people to see. Ethan had introduced him to his coworkers, they had mingled, drank, eaten. It'd been pretty much like any other job.

Except the part where he said he liked me. That's what he said, wasn't it?

Had he misheard? Felix thought back to the strange things Ethan had said when he'd first shown up at the

Christmas party. Ethan had sprung on him, pulled him into a kiss, and had said *like*, hadn't he? As quick as Ethan had said it, he was pulling Felix toward a group of people and introducing him as his boyfriend as contracted.

It's supposed to be pretend. They'd both been drinking, and he was confused about what he was feeling. Ethan confused him.

The way Ethan kissed him had seemed a little too aggressive to have just been for show, but then, when the Daniel thing had been explained, it made sense. A few of the people they'd talked to had seemed a bit awkward at first, but, as far as Felix was concerned, the night had gone well. He felt something for Ethan—wanted to be near him, wanted to touch him.

His chest felt heavy. He didn't understand what he was feeling. Or what he was supposed to do about those feelings.

Felix hadn't been with someone in a long time. His last boyfriend had been controlling, but their relationship hadn't been all bad. *At least I didn't think so.* But there had been something there, a pressure in his gut when they were together. *Sometimes, I felt as if I couldn't breathe.* With Ethan, it was different, and there was an easiness between them, and a heat Felix wouldn't mind taking a step further.

"Come on." He shook away the old memories and turned to hook his arm in Ethan's. He said, "You don't want to miss your train."

At the station, they stood together on the platform, waiting for Ethan's train to arrive.

"Will you be okay by yourself?" Felix asked. Once he saw Ethan on the train, he'd flag down a taxi to take him back to his apartment.

"I'll be fine. Thank you." Ethan folded his arms across his chest and leaned over to look past Felix and down the line. "If you want to go, you can. My train should be here soon."

Felix shook his head. "I'm good." He nuzzled his chin beneath the collar of his coat. "As you said, it'll be here soon." He met Ethan's eyes. Neither of them spoke. They stared into each other's eyes until the sound of the incoming train broke the spell. Felix felt like a coward for not talking about the kisses and the words and the—

"Here it is," Ethan interrupted his thoughts. He hunched his shoulders and moved nearer to the edge of the platform.

"Yeah," Felix uttered. There it was. He joined Ethan as he waited to board. "So, goodnight." He hesitated, then pulled Ethan into a brief hug. He breathed in as they parted and smiled. "Get home safe."

"Thanks." The door to the carriage opened, and Ethan stepped inside. "Night."

Felix stepped back, ducking his head as he tried to spy Ethan through the carriage windows as he took a seat. Regret twinged through his heart. Maybe he should've brought up what Ethan had said before.

The train pulled away.

Too late now.

Nearly had it.

Felix stared at the wooden puzzle piece. He had no idea where it was supposed to fit. While Ethan had been gifted edible body paint, Felix had received a pair of 3D geometric puzzles from the secret Santa at Ethan's department party a few nights ago.

Maybe I should have swapped for the chocolate paint.

He dismantled the 3D cross he had been building and spread the pieces out on the dining table. With a sigh, he started over.

"Still struggling with this thing?" his mom said as she rolled up beside him. She picked up one of the pieces and tapped it on the tabletop.

"Hmm." He took the piece from her. "I can't decide if I'm having fun or not. It's a little bit frustrating."

Karin gave a soft chuckle. "You'll figure it out eventually. Or find a loophole."

Felix looked at her. "What are you talking about?"

"You were only little. You had one of those buckets with different-shaped holes in the lid. You were supposed to fit the shapes to the right holes to get them inside."

"Ah, I know the toy you mean."

"Turned out you could pretty much push every shape through one of the holes. You looked so pleased with yourself."

Felix laughed. "Work smart, not hard."

Karin rubbed his arm. "Are you okay? You look tired."

Felix raised his shoulders. "I'm fine. It's just been busy at work as it's the run-up to Christmas. Lots to do."

"Are you sure? If coming round here is too much for you, then—"

"Mom, I'm fine." He rested his hand over hers. "Promise. Besides it won't be for much longer. Then, I'll get out of your and Dad's way."

"Hey, now you're making me feel bad. We've loved seeing more of you. I just don't like the idea of burdening you with our problems."

He leaned over and hugged her. "As if I'd think that." He pressed a kiss to her cheek. "Honestly, I'm fine." He fiddled with one of the puzzle pieces. As well as being busy at work, he was distracted by not one, but two puzzles. One, the wooden cross, the other his heart. He wasn't going to tell his mom that, though. She didn't need to know about Ethan and how he'd been in his thoughts the last few days.

Not yet.

"Okay, I believe you." She squeezed his arm. "Are you staying for supper?"

Felix shook his head. "Not tonight. I'm meeting work friends for a drink, and then, I'll head back to my place. I've nothing organized for tomorrow, so I'll swing by later in the day. I might treat myself and sleep in."

"You mean you plan on getting drunk?"

He grinned. "Maybe that, too."

"If you want to stay home tomorrow you can." She stroked his forearm with her thumb. "We'll manage for a day."

A lazy day sounded nice. "I'll think about it." But he was usually happiest when he was keeping busy. He leaned to bump his shoulder to hers. "I'll see what time I wake up." He winked.

Karin pressed her hand to his cheek. "Don't drink too much." She smiled.

"I won't."

"Felix," Jared called out when Felix entered the bar.

Felix raised a hand, acknowledging he had seen him. He slipped through a crowd of people and joined Jared at a table in the corner. "Hey." He stopped, surprised to find Ethan sitting with him, tucked in the corner. "Oh, Ethan. I didn't know you were coming."

"Not willingly," Ethan grumbled.

Felix laughed. "Okay." He slid into the seat next to Jared and asked, "What did you do to him?"

Jared rested his head in his hand. "I saved him from an ocean of Post-it notes. He was driving himself crazy working on something." He shared a glance with Ethan, who went to say something, but backed down. "I thought a break was in order."

Narrowing his eyes, Felix looked between the two of them. "Right. Well, a break is always good." He shrugged off his jacket. "Is Nate joining us?" He checked the bar. "Is he in tonight?"

"Luka has a school project to finish before Christmas break. Nate sends his apologies, but he needs to stay home and lend a hand. Caleb's coming in later, but only if his date doesn't go late."

"Does Caleb ever stop?" Felix sighed. "Last time I

worked with him, he was talking about taking a second job."

"Yeah. He needs a night off, and he says he'll try his hardest to be here." Jared pointed at his bottle of beer. "What do you want to drink?"

"Beer's fine."

Jared went to stand, but it was Ethan who jumped to his feet. "I'll get them," he insisted and strolled away before anyone could disagree.

"Is he okay?" Felix asked.

"Who?"

"Ethan."

"Oh," Jared said, "ignore him. He's fine. Wired on equations and overthinking." He twisted his drink by the bottle neck. "Have you been okay? I presume the Christmas party went without a hitch?"

Felix nodded. "Didn't Ethan say anything?"

"Not specifically about that, but he did talk to me about what happened after the reunion."

"He did?"

"Said you kissed him," Jared prompted, but Felix knew that it wasn't Jared he needed to talk to, but Ethan himself. "But that's between the two of you, so…" He shrugged. "Anyway, I went over to the apartment this afternoon to find Ethan dazed and confused on the couch, hypothesizing." He leaned in closer. "Not sure what about though."

He may or may not have confessed to liking me. No way in hell he was bringing that up. Felix glanced over to the bar where Ethan was being served. "I don't know either."

"Hmm." Jared sat back, narrowed his eyes as he stared at Felix.

There was a warning in Jared's gaze—break my friend and I'll break you—but it wasn't necessary. He'd felt off balance since the Christmas party, a little lost, and the craving for more kisses, or just to see Ethan again, was fierce.

They were interrupted by Ethan returning with drinks, and when he began to ramble about the whiskey-making process as soon as he sat down, it was the perfect excuse to listen and not have to think at all. When it was his turn to get drinks, he headed for the restroom first, anything to get away from the fact that Caleb, fellow boyfriend for hire, had arrived and was currently talking Ethan's ear off about stem cell research. *I'm not jealous. He's not mine.*

"Felix!" Ethan exclaimed as they came face-to-face as he exited the restroom, Felix still lost in thought.

"Sorry," Felix said and stepped around Ethan, expecting him to go past into the bathroom.

"Wait." Ethan grabbed him by the wrist. "Um…"

Felix moved to one side so as not to block the door. Ethan followed him, and they stood against the wall. "Is everything okay?" He waited; Ethan seemed agitated.

"Well…"

Maybe I should go first. "Ethan, about the other night—"

"I need one more favor."

Felix flinched as Ethan met his eyes with a determined expression. "Erm, okay. What?"

"I'm sorry. I know it's troublesome, but can you

pretend to be my boyfriend again?" He scratched the back of his head, ruffling his hair. "I'll tell everyone we broke up in the New Year, so I promise this is the last time."

The last time? Why did his chest ache at those words?

"Assuming I'm available, I don't see why not. Is it the engagement party you mentioned or…"

Ethan sighed. "It's my family."

"'Family'?"

"Mom and Dad usually go on vacation for Christmas, so we have a family meal the week before." He rested a hand on his hip. "Julian and those damn pictures. My sister saw them, and so now, everyone wants to meet you."

"At the family meal?"

Ethan nodded. "She and my brother always bring their partners. I never have. In fact, I don't think my family have met any of my previous boyfriends."

"So why now?"

"Because of Julian's photos." He pouted. "My previous relationships have hardly been worth shouting about. I never told them anything even if they asked. It's the first time they've had irrefutable evidence of me dating someone." He huffed. "Julian," he muttered.

Felix couldn't help but laugh. Ethan was so damn cute when he was grumpy. "Okay. I'll do it."

"Really?"

"As I said, assuming I'm available. Text me the date in case I forget, and I'll check it as soon as I can."

Ethan seemed relieved. "You're a lifesaver. I'll get in touch with Rowan and—"

"No need."

"What?"

"You don't need to go through Rowan." He met Ethan's eyes, considered saying more.

He found Ethan interesting and was drawn to his quirky character. There was a definite attraction, and he had found himself enjoying the dates they had spent together, even if they had been paid for.

But they barely knew each other.

I don't think I'm ready to make any grand statement.

The only way to know was to spend more time with him.

He pulled Ethan into a hug and said, "I want to help." He smiled when he felt Ethan's arms around his waist, squeezing him back.

"Thank you," Ethan said.

Felix closed his eyes, enjoyed the lingering hug. Ethan's body was warm against his. "You're welcome."

Chapter Ten

You don't need to go through Rowan.

The words made Ethan's head spin, and he didn't know what to do with his feelings. On the one hand, guilt consumed him that he was asking Felix to do yet more favors for him, but on the other, he wanted to spend as much time with his sexy fake boyfriend as he could. He didn't want to read too much into the fact that Felix said they didn't need to go through Rowan, but it left him confused. If they weren't going through Rowan, then who did Ethan pay? They were already halfway to his parents' house in Amesbury, and the thorny issue of payment was sitting at the front of Ethan's thoughts.

Right alongside his sad ones about how he wished this was a *real* date.

He knew he needed to bring up the subject of money before his brain imploded and he became even more awkward. But how to do that? He couldn't sit here and message Jared to ask about what to do without making things too obvious, and also because it was rude to ignore Felix and spend all his time on his phone. So, he defaulted to working out a complete list of conversation openers; from ones where he asked Felix how he was supposed to pay him in a direct way, to others where he asked the perfect leading question, which encouraged Felix to offer the information on his own.

"You okay over there?" Felix asked, as Google's directions instructed they take the next exit. Ethan began analyzing this new route, thinking ahead to the typical issues on the turnpike. Two Christmases ago, after a sudden dumping of snow, he and Jared had gotten trapped at the same exit that the navigation was telling them to use. Stuck for three hours waiting to be rescued hadn't been fun, and Ethan peered out of the window, checking the dense stratocumulus clouds, just in case.

"It might snow." As if to underscore what he said, a few flakes danced around them.

Felix chuckled. "The forecast said snow, but we should be in Amesbury before it gets bad. What are the roads like near your folks' place?"

Ethan latched onto the first part of what Felix said. If Felix was okay to talk about snow, then maybe Ethan could shelve the payment worries and talk to his traveling companion, who'd volunteered to drive and everything, about the weather. He didn't know everything there was to know about meteorology, but he knew enough about altostratus clouds to carry a conversation.

"Earth to Ethan, come in Ethan? What are the roads like?"

Jeez, in all of that thought processing, it seemed he'd missed a question. "Sorry?"

"The roads?

"What about them?"

Felix sent him a fond look. "The ones near your parents' house? Will they be okay if this snow gets heavier?"

Ethan blinked at Felix, making sense of this new question in among everything else he was thinking about. "They're not far off the main road, and my brother will be there to help shovel the drive for us." He then subsided into silence, twisting his fingers in his lap, knowing he needed to ask for confirmation of payment because that was all he could think about, and it was taking up so much of his brain he couldn't even answer questions.

"Tell me a bit about your family?" Felix prompted.

Oh yeah, I forgot to brief him.

Stop thinking about money and focus on the job at hand. Maybe if he started this booking off with the same level of detail Rowan had wanted for the first one, then the money thing would just get mentioned.

"Well, there's my brother, Sean. He's younger than me by a year, and my sister Claire, she's the oldest of all three of us. Sean is an electrician, and his wife is Emma. Um, my sister has a long-term boyfriend, Erik. She met him way back in kindergarten, and they've been together ever since. Mom messaged me to say that she thinks he might propose at New Year's. What else do you need to know? Oh, Sean has two children, both girls, Maisie, and Charlotte, and they're expecting a third in the spring. Mom went back to being a legal assistant after all of us were finally in school. She works in an office in town. Dad is a librarian, and they've been married thirty-two years. Is that enough to give you an idea of what to expect?" Ethan was nervous that he'd somehow let his emotions color what he was saying. His family was important to him, and to have to distill everything he felt for them down to dry facts was near impossible.

"So, do your siblings live close to your parents?"

"Yep, Sean does. After we were all done with high school, Mom and Dad moved to be nearer to family. Claire and I went off to college and Sean came with them to Amesbury. Sean opted out of going onto further education, so never left, built a life there, and Claire, after completing her degree in early childhood education, decided to go home to where we grew up. She had Erik there. Actually, she's a teacher at the same school we went to as kids. Full circle." Shit, that was a profound end to the statement—yet more personal stuff not to be included in a family overview.

"That sounds perfect. You're a close family, then?"

"We are. It's hard for them to have to put up with me when I'm in my head most of the time. They tease me, but it's kind, because I tease them back. They all have ordinary IQs, you see?"

Felix smiled. "They do?"

"That came out wrong, didn't it—I don't mean I tease them for their intelligence. Jeez, no. I meant...

god, I don't know what I mean. I love them, and they are perfect, and they never make me feel like it's wrong to want to fix things in the world. Or to forget to call them on a Sunday. Or to never bring home a boy who means anything to me." He bit his lip. Had he revealed too much there? Felix had grown to mean something to him. Something beyond the fact he'd been hired to be here, but it wasn't as if he could tell him that. He bet everyone Felix dated fell for him, with his kindness, and his perfect PDAs, and his beautiful smile, and his gorgeous eyes. No wonder people wanted to book Felix.

Talking about booked—Ethan's thoughts spiraled again, and he sunk into his seat, and rested his head on the window, staring out at the falling snow and passing road signs, until the first sign for the turnoff appeared. Then, thoughts of money changed to memories of the Christmas two years ago.

"You're very quiet. Is everything okay? If you want to change the music, you can."

"I wasn't listening to the music," Ethan admitted, and then frowned at the road, a few flakes swirling down from a leaden sky.

"You look thoughtful. Are you worried about going home?"

"No, not at all. I was remembering two Christmases ago when Jared was driving us to my parents, and there was a snowstorm. We got caught on the off-ramp and we were stuck there for three hours, until these recovery guys came and pulled us out of the snow." The clouds didn't look heavy enough for that to happen again. Their journey snacks comprised a large bag of mini Kit-

Kats, half a bag of Sour Patch Kids, and two bottles of soda. Not the healthiest haul if they got stuck. At least they had coats. Plus, Ethan had spotted blankets in the back of the car when he'd put his bag in there, and they could always snuggle for warmth.

Ethan glanced at Felix, who side-eyed him, accompanied by a soft smile. "Tell me everything—even better if the story ends with Jared falling into the snowdrift."

"He didn't."

"Shame." Felix chuckled.

That was all the encouragement Ethan needed to expand on the story, and not think about money at all.

"There was this recovery driver—Sid, I think his name was. He was a great guy, and I remember he was trying to find this special gift for his daughter for Christmas, and he was all upset that he was going to let his daughter down. It was like the start of a movie where he ends up trying to get a toy, and he has to fight Arnold Schwarzenegger or something to get it. At least, I think that was the movie. Have you seen the movie? Probably not, it's an old one, and Arnie looks young. Or was that the picture I have of him in my head from a *Terminator* film? I don't know. Has there ever been snow in a *Terminator* film? I think the first one, when he arrives naked. Hell, he looked good naked. I should look it up."

By the time Ethan finished rambling about everything and nothing, Felix had not only taken the off-ramp, but he'd parked and killed the engine, and when Ethan took a breath, he saw golden arches and a gas station. He wriggled in his seat and turned to face Felix.

"Do we need gas? Let me get this because we haven't talked about how I'm paying you, and it's all in my head about what this means, and why you said we shouldn't involve Rowan, and I'm not sure—"

He never got to finish explaining the rest of his thought process, because Felix cradled his face, leaned over at an awkward angle, and kissed the words right out of his mouth. As distractions went, this was the best one Ethan had ever experienced, and he tried his hardest not to overthink the situation. But why was Felix kissing him when there was no one here to impress? Well, aside from Ethan—who was very impressed. Felix deepened the kiss, tilting his head, and all Ethan could do was go along for the ride, determined that this kiss would never end.

Until it did.

Felix eased back, and Ethan chased for more, opening his eyes and finding that they were a few inches apart.

"What was that for?" He didn't remember asking for a kiss in all his rambling, but maybe at some point, he'd implied that a kiss would make everything better? Only it hadn't made things better. He was still confused, but at least he'd now been kissed by someone who knew what they were doing. Felix's kisses were addictive—even if they were fake.

"I just felt like it." Felix smiled, closed the short distance between them, and pressed a kiss to the end of Ethan's nose. "You were all cute—telling me a story about Sid, and Arnold, and snow—and I just got this feeling that I needed to kiss you."

"But there's no one here to see a PDA." Ethan waved out of the window at the near-empty parking lot.

Felix chuckled. "I'll let you think about that one."

Wait, Felix was asking Ethan to think about why he stopped the car and then kissed him? If it wasn't because they needed a PDA for people to see, and if Felix said that he found Ethan cute with his rambling stories that went nowhere, then the only solution to that equation was that Felix *wanted* to kiss him, just for the sake of it.

"Oh," Ethan mumbled. There was no other reason —no other solution to the confusion at hand. "The only conclusion I have is that you *wanted* to kiss me. You said I'm cute, so you wanted to kiss me because I'm cute?"

"There you go."

"Wow, thank you. I like kissing you, too," Ethan murmured after a pause. "I don't think you're cute, though. I mean, I do, but in a hot, sexy way." He could feel heat and knew he must be scarlet. "Ignore I said that. I'll miss kissing you when it's over. Unless, of course, you could just come round to my workplace, or my apartment, and sell me a kiss for a few dollars now and then?"

Felix rolled his eyes. "How about, instead of me showing up for emergency kisses, I take you out for dinner, we talk about ourselves to each other, and end the night with more kisses?"

"But you won't make much money doing it that way? Unless I pay for dinner, because then I guess, you're not paying, and so you get a free meal? I'm good with that if it means I get more kisses at the end.

Although, McDonald's might be as far as I can go in terms of food, because you know money is tight with everything, and I—"

Felix kissed him again, and this time, Ethan laced his fingers behind Felix's head and refused to let go. Each kiss was deep, and searching, and so freaking hot, and he didn't want them to stop.

Still, they had to breathe; but when Felix eased away, Ethan refused to untangle his fingers, just in case there was another kiss.

"Ethan, I don't think you're understanding this. I don't *need* payment for kisses that I want," Felix whispered and rested his forehead against Ethan's.

"You *want* to kiss me? As much as I want to kiss you?" Ethan wasn't sure why he asked that question. Maybe it was years of never being sure where he stood in a relationship, or whether a partner really wanted everything he had to give. So many of them laughed at him for the way his squirrel brain darted in different directions, some of them didn't want to kiss—and kissing was the best part of everything, alongside waking up on a cold, frosty morning, cuddled in blankets, with someone you loved holding you close.

Love? No. Do not *get in my brain.*

Felix smiled. "Yes, I want to kiss you as much as you want to kiss me."

Okay, all that seemed like a solid statement. Still, Ethan had to make sure Felix knew he wasn't taking him for a ride. "I don't want you to think that I'm trying not to pay you, but… I'm confused. You said we shouldn't go through Rowan, and I don't know how else I'm supposed to give you the money that I owe you."

Felix closed his eyes, and then stole another kiss, which Ethan enthusiastically went along with. He was addicted to Felix's kisses, that much was sure, and he knew he'd feel bereft when he couldn't have them anymore.

"Let's go outside for a minute," Felix suggested, and even though it was bitter out in the open, they wrapped up in coats and hovered by the car. Ethan considered all the facts he knew about wind chill—anything to avoid him saying anything stupid—but then, he lost all rational thought when Felix pressed him back against the car and cradled his face. Pinned to the cold metal, he melted in Felix's hold, and there was no time for shivering when Felix started the hottest kiss of Ethan's entire life. Ethan's world shifted, tilted on its axis, his heart beating fast, and he was so hard. He wished he could climb inside Felix's coat and stay snuggled in there forever.

"I love kissing you," Felix murmured against Ethan's lips, and then smiled. "And the reason we're not going through Rowan is because this isn't a booking. Okay?"

Ethan considered all the evidence—the fact they were kissing in a McDonald's parking lot, that he could feel how turned-on Felix was, and in the soft words Felix had given him. For the first time in his life, he didn't want to solve an equation by balancing all the variables. This time, he needed the answer to be given to him.

"Then what is it?" he asked.

"I'm not sure," Felix admitted, kissed him again, and

eased away. "But it feels very much like a real first date to me."

"Oh!" Something eased inside Ethan, his knotted worries unraveling, and his thoughts settled. "Oh," he repeated, and this time, it was he who started the next kiss.

They made it to his parents' place a little after four. His entire family crowded into his space as soon as he set foot through the front door, a cacophony of questions, interspersed with hugs from his mom, dad, sister, brother, and nieces. Felix stood next to him, taking in just as many hugs, and he did so without flinching once.

And through all of that first chaos in the hallway, Felix held his hand.

Chapter Eleven

Did I overdo it earlier?

Felix was full of food and relaxed, and his thoughts drifted to earlier and the kisses both inside and outside the car. Ethan had been on one of his cute rambles and a strong urge had overtaken Felix. He'd wanted to grab hold of him and kiss him silly. It had just been a thought, but then, Ethan had brought up money.

I wanted to stop him asking about money.

He hadn't offered to be Ethan's boyfriend tonight for a paycheck, he wanted to spend time with him, to help him, to see into his world a little more. A family dinner seemed one way to do that.

But then we kissed more, and it felt good. Kissing Ethan had been easy, so easy it had led him to suggesting maybe there was something real between them. *A real first date. I did say that.*

Felix glanced at Ethan. They hadn't had any time to themselves since reaching Ethan's parents' home. In some ways, he was glad. Watching Ethan spend time with family was eye-opening. Felix didn't think he had seen Ethan smile as much as he had tonight. It seemed he really did enjoy being in his family's presence—from his parents to his nieces. Ethan slipped easily between devoted son, big brother, and heart-eyed uncle when with the two girls. Ethan's cuteness could take more than one form, but Ethan being in his own head and going off at tangents-cute was Felix's favorite. He found the habit charming.

"I don't think we should," Ethan's mother said as she rejoined the group around the dining table. Though various members of the family and Felix himself had offered to clear up after the meal, Anita had insisted they stay seated.

Felix blinked and refocused on the conversation at the table. He glanced at his hand in Ethan's. Their fingers were intertwined, and Ethan's palm was warm against his. Their interactions had become natural and easy over the course of the evening. He was getting used to the feel of Ethan's hand in his.

"Come on, Mom. It'll be fun," said Claire. She grunted as she lifted one of her nieces onto her lap.

Anita shook her head. "You say that now, but you know at least one of you will be sulking before the evening ends."

Sean said with a chuckle, "Yeah, usually Ethan."

Ah, I completely missed what they're talking about.

Ethan breathed in, as if he were about to defend himself, but instead, he said in a solemn tone, "He's correct."

Sean was sitting on the other side of Ethan and

patted his shoulder gently. He leaned forward to speak to Felix. "His favorite square is *go to jail*."

So, they're talking about Monopoly.

Sean smirked as he stared at Ethan.

With a sigh, Ethan said, "Also correct."

Felix chuckled. "I suppose you can't science your way through a game mostly based on the luck of dice rolls."

"Trust me, he tried," said Sean. "Sadly, for him, knowing the probability of rolling a seven doesn't mean it's going to happen."

"It doesn't help you buy everything you land on," Ethan pointed out.

Sean sat back. "That's the fun part."

"So, that's a no for Monopoly?" Claire checked. She bounced her knees, jiggling her niece and making her laugh. "How about something the kids can play too?"

Sean's wife stood. "It's okay, you can play whatever you want. The girls are going to watch a movie." She held out her hand. "Come on, Maisie. Let's go pick something with your sister."

Maisie hopped off Claire's lap and went to her mother, taking her hand as they left the dining room.

The remaining family members slipped into silence for a moment before Claire spoke up. "Monopoly?"

A couple of people groaned.

Ethan said, "Feel free, but we'll probably not stay for much longer, as we need to drive back."

"Tonight?" Sean asked. "You're not staying over?"

Ethan shook his head. "Not this year."

"My fault," Felix said and raised his hand. "I need to

go back."

One night probably wouldn't have been a problem as far as his parents were concerned, but Felix still felt uneasy at the thought of being away for extended periods of time, at least until his dad was completely healed. Ethan had decided that he would return as well. He could have easily stayed with his family for longer, but it seemed he was happy either way, and decided he wanted to keep Felix company on the drive back.

"Maybe next time?" Anita said with a smile. She shifted her focus to Felix as she added, "You're welcome anytime."

"Thank you," Felix said. "It's been great to meet you all."

"You, too. You know, Ethan never introduces us to any of his boyfriends. It was a lovely surprise when he said he was bringing you tonight."

"Mom," Ethan whined.

"What? It's true. Not even once." She folded her arms. "I wouldn't have even known you'd dated anyone at all, if not for Jared."

"Jared?" Felix asked.

"Mmm. I called Ethan one night, and Jared hadn't realized Ethan was talking to me and started talking about this boyfriend who'd left his towel on the floor, again, so I might have heard a few things."

"Ah." Felix was sure Jared had gotten a telling-off over that.

Ethan huffed a breath. "As I said, we weren't that serious, so I didn't see the point in telling you about him." He glanced at Felix. "Not that we are——" He shut up and winced. "What I mean is, well, we just started dating so…" He looked at his mom. "Besides, you and Claire wouldn't shut up about those reunion photos, so it's not as if you left me much choice but to bring him." He scratched behind his ear. "I really should review my settings on these things and who can see stuff and tag stuff and—" Felix squeezed his hand, and he stopped talking.

"Stop being so dramatic." Claire said with a smirk. "We only asked if you wanted to bring him along." She turned to Felix. "Seriously, we asked him maybe three times." She chuckled and added, "Each."

"You kept ignoring my messages," Anita said to Ethan. "And I needed to know how many people to expect for dinner." Her expression was gentle. "Those pictures from the reunion were lovely though. Everybody seemed to be having fun. Must have been nice to catch up with people."

Nice? Felix felt tense all of a sudden. He and Ethan hadn't spoken about the reunion or anything that had happened. *I don't want to bring up anything unnecessary.* He only wanted to see Ethan smile. Just as he had been doing tonight. He smoothed his thumb over Ethan's wrist. His tension eased when the conversation moved on.

Claire jumped in, "I think I remember Julian who tagged you. He came over a few times back at the old house, didn't he?"

"Yes," Ethan said with a smile. "We paired up most of the time when we had papers to write." Ethan seemed fine.

I was worrying over nothing.

The conversation continued for another forty minutes until Ethan decided it was time to excuse themselves.

"I think that went okay," Ethan said a short while into the journey home.

"Mmm." Felix focused on the road as he drove slowly, following at a distance the car in front of him. At least it wasn't snowing, and the roads were clear. "Your family all seem nice."

Ethan shifted in the passenger seat. "I think they are."

Felix was relieved. Not everyone had a loving family around them, supporting them.

"What about you?"

"Hmm? Me, what?"

"Your family. You haven't really told me much about them."

Felix gripped the steering wheel. "There's nothing much to say really." He couldn't remember what details he had shared as preparation for the school reunion, and they had only come up once that evening, when Ethan's dad had asked about Christmas, if and how Felix celebrated and with whom. "It's just me, Mom, and Dad."

"Right," Ethan said.

"Dad has family in Salem, but we're not close." He paused. "It's more of a Christmas card, weddings, and funerals kind of thing." He leaned forward when the car in front braked, it and the vehicles in the other lanes slowing together. It didn't make sense at first, and then a few flakes of snow fell on the hood. People overreacting as usual. He relaxed a little, adding, "Mom has some close friends I call auntie and uncle. They get together now and again, usually on birthdays."

"Right," Ethan said again. He stayed quiet for a while, then noted, "It's snowing."

A few more flakes fell, but it wasn't exactly Snowmageddon, yet everyone was braking, and the car stopped just short of the turnoff for a motel.

"We could stop for a coffee?" Ethan murmured. "Get back on the road when the traffic starts to move?" He was staring at his phone and the map app on there. "It's red for the next five miles, an accident I think."

"Would you be okay with that?" Felix checked. "We could keep going, slowly, but we might as well get a coffee?"

Ethan shrugged. "I'm not the one driving. You decide."

Thoughts of his parents came to the forefront. As much as he wanted to be home and close by if anything came up, the traffic wasn't moving, and unless they went back twenty or more miles to the last turnoff and went cross-country, they were pretty balked right now.

Making the decision, Felix put his blinkers on and turned off the road. He parked and turned off the engine. He and Ethan sat together for a short moment and considered the rest area and the motel.

"What do you want to do?" Ethan asked. The snow had picked up, a swirling mess of white that blocked their view of the motel sign.

"Maybe I should get back on the road? If it keeps

snowing like this…" Wind buffeted the car, and an icy blast rocked them. At least they were off the road and not stuck out there with the rest of the traffic, because if it kept snowing like this, then being on the freeway wouldn't be fun. "Does it say anything about the weather?"

"Freak storm, blah blah, accident, blah blah." Ethan glanced at him worriedly. "We should have left earlier; I'm sorry." A few more cars joined them in the parking area, then a couple more, and the parking lot was filling quickly.

"Do we get a coffee and wait to see if it stops or…" His gaze was on the motel.

"Give up and get a room?" Felix finished for him. People were hurrying to the front door of the tiny motel, and he watched the snow settling on the front of the car. Was it going to stop any time soon?

"Screw it," he said. "Let's just get a room for the night. It's pretty late anyway. It's probably better to sleep than drive tired in this weather. Would you be okay with that?" He met Ethan's eyes.

Ethan bit on his lower lip. He nodded. "I'd be okay with that." There was a shift in Ethan's tone, and Felix was left not wanting to turn away.

Had Ethan really needed to sound that seductive? And what the hell was with that lip-bite?

Felix cleared his throat, zipped up his jacket. There were no belongings to grab, so after checking that he had his cell phone and wallet secured, he got out of the car.

So cold. He hunched up his shoulders as he waited for

Ethan to exit the car, then together they made their way through the snow and to the motel. After the others on the road had called it quits on their journeys, too, he and Ethan found themselves in a line, with other people who were all talking dramatically about what they'd turned off to avoid.

"Heard a truck jackknifed…"

"Blocked for hours…"

"Snow…"

All in all, it seemed they'd made the right decision. There was a chance to get two rooms, but the queue was long behind them, so it made sense to share—Felix didn't even think about the only one bed thing—or at least he did, but he was determined not to be that guy, because Ethan didn't seem worried at all. They could easily keep their hands off each other, take things slow—maybe talk chemistry equations from opposite sides of the bed.

After a short wait, they were able to get a room and were checked in for the night.

"Oh, it's nice and warm in here," Ethan said as he kicked off his shoes, then shuffled inside to make way for Felix.

Felix shut the door, shook the last of the snow from his hair, and shrugged off his jacket. He glanced at Ethan, who had taken a seat on the end of the huge bed. Some pillows down the center and it would be absolutely fine. *I won't kiss Ethan. I won't roll over accidentally in my sleep and snuggle him. I'm a grown-ass man. I have control.* "I guess this will do us for tonight."

Ethan smiled. "I guess."

Felix toed off his shoes. He stood for a moment, his eyes on Ethan. He swallowed, his mind not missing the fact it was the two of them, alone, sharing a bed for the night. "Erm." He brushed back his bangs. "I need to make a quick call. Is that okay?"

"Of course."

Felix headed to the back of the room and into the bathroom. He pushed the door closed, leaving a small gap. Pulling out his cell phone, he first contacted Jared.

"My parents have your number so, though I'm sure it won't be necessary for them to use it, but if anything comes up will you be okay to handle it?"

"Of course," Jared said. "And you take care of Ethan for me."

"Will do."

"Did you get one room or two?"

"One, there were so many people lining up, families too—"

"One room, one bed…"

Was that a warning? Was Jared warning him not to mess with Ethan? "That's not a thing," he muttered, but Jared ended the call after a snort of laughter. Clearly, not a warning then. Asshole.

He then went on to call his mom, explaining in length about the accident, the snow, the motel, and she didn't stop him.

"I'm glad you're safe," his mom said when he took a breath. "Thanks for letting us know."

"Everything's okay, yes?" He needed to be there. What if his mom needed him, and his dad couldn't help?

"Of course, it is."

Felix leaned back against the basin. "I've let Jared know, so if anything does happen, you can call him. Do you need his phone number again or…"

"We have it. So, stop worrying and go get some rest, okay?"

"Yes, Mom," Felix said with a chuckle. "I'll see you soon."

"Sure, baby. Be safe."

"You, too. Bye for now."

"Night."

He let his mom hang up first, then straightened. He left the bathroom to find Ethan where he had left him, sitting on the foot of the bed.

"Finished?" Ethan looked up at him.

"Yes." He joined Ethan and sat next to him. He rested his hand on the comforter, his fingers within reach of Ethan's. With a sigh, he stared around the room, trying to decide where to settle his attention. He was surprised when Ethan rested his hand over his.

"Are you okay?" he asked.

"Yes." Ethan flicked his tongue over his bottom lip. His lifted his gaze. "Are you?"

Their eyes met and Felix was hit by a wave of desire. Ethan's gaze was intense. It was as if he were waiting for the answer to an, as of yet, unspoken question.

Ethan tilted his head slightly, leaning closer. What was going through his head? Was it the same thoughts, feelings as Felix? Because the only thought Felix had right then was…

I want to kiss him.

Chapter Twelve

Ethan could blame the truck jackknifing, or the snow, or the fact he and Felix were in a hotel room with only one bed, but whatever it was, he was torn between wanting to kiss him and wanting to run. In this moment, it didn't matter why they were in this room. All he knew was that he wanted Felix so badly, and he was hot, and his heart pounded, and his chest was tight.

And yeah, he wanted to leave before he fucked things up.

"Ethan? Are you okay?" Felix sounded worried—distant, as if he was asking from across the room.

Ethan was as far from okay as was possible. He didn't know how to do this. He inevitably messed up everything from talking too much, kissing too hard, or going straight to his knees. Sex wasn't about him, or for him, because he didn't…

Didn't what? Deserve it? Was he good enough for someone to be with? He'd gone to the prom, thinking maybe the cute kid from the library—whose name he didn't recall now—would want to dance with him. Maybe even kiss him. And all that had happened was the bathroom incident. He'd never gotten what he thought he wanted, and had he really resigned himself to never having that kiss or something more? Why did he do this to himself? He was like every other red-blooded male, and surely, with a bit of practice, he could be just as good as the next man at this sex thing? He removed his hand from where he was touching Felix. Maybe the best thing would be to enjoy the moment of want, and not let it go any further. Then, there was no chance of him messing up.

"Are you okay?" Felix was frowning in confusion, or was that disappointment and horror? Ethan had seen how Felix leaned in, ready to kiss him, but then what? Kisses led to sex. Sex was over in the blink of an eye. Then, they would be in that awkward moment where Felix realized Ethan was too much, or not right for him, or was too loud, too messy, too much in his head—

"Earth to Ethan? What's wrong?" Felix reached for Ethan's hand, but before there was contact Ethan slid off the bed, stumbled, then headed for the door, his fingers wrapping around the handle. "You're worrying me," Felix stood. "Do you need something?"

"Yes!" Ethan blurted. "I need that!" He pointed at the bed, and then at himself. "But I really like you, Felix, and if we do *that*, five minutes in, you'll be done—I'll be done—and that's it. It's all over. I've messed up; you're disappointed; and I'll keep talking, and then you'll just leave because I'm just too much. Why do you think I'm single? Why do you think I can't get a date who actually sticks with me? I'm all over the fucking place. I can't keep my focus when I'm in a relationship. Not that I have them. I don't do what people think I should do."

"Ethan—"

"So, I think probably the best thing for you and me, is for me to book another room, and we'll meet at breakfast. Then, we can go back to the city and pretend this hasn't happened, and we'll go back to being friends. I could use friends because it's not fair that Jared carries the entire burden of me."

Felix blinked slowly, and Ethan could almost imagine Felix's horror as he processed all the nonsense that had just tumbled out of his mouth. He turned the handle, ready to step outside and hide in the hallway, giving in to the complete mortification that was him overthinking everything.

"Okay," Felix murmured, and Ethan's heart sank. Had he somehow talked himself out of sex? Or making love, which is what he'd thought this might have been. Regrets knocked him sideways, and then he felt as if he wanted to cry, because yet again he'd misread the situation, overreacted, and made a fool of himself.

"So, yeah, okay," Ethan agreed with himself. "I'll see you at breakfast."

Felix was off the bed in an instant, stepping between Ethan and the door, and unpeeling Ethan's fingers from the handle.

"Sit down." Felix pointed to the chair in the corner, which looked all kinds of soft, warm, and inviting.

"I don't think that—"

"Sit down. For me."

The distance between the door and the chair was only six steps, which would take him away from Felix, but then he'd be stuck in the corner, with no way out. All he could imagine was that Felix wanted him to talk, but right now, he didn't want to talk about the mess in his head. Or about closing doors as Jared did, or about what had happened at the reunion. Or about the fact that he'd just had the best time with his family, and they all loved Felix. His mom had whispered in his ear, *"Don't let this one go"*. All Ethan could do was nod at that and pretend to agree.

Felix wasn't his to let go.

"Sit," Felix commanded, and there was something in his tone that meant Ethan didn't argue. He tried his hardest to get to the chair without falling over, and that took all his brainpower, until he perched on the edge of the seat. He settled his breathing and glanced up at Felix.

"Five minutes?" Felix murmured. "For real?"

Ethan didn't understand the question. Then, he couldn't think of anything at all. Felix slipped off the button-down he was wearing over a T-shirt. He'd already taken off his coat and winter weather layers, the same as Ethan had.

"Five minutes?" Felix repeated.

Ethan wasn't sure why Felix had said that twice because it wasn't a question, or a comment, and Ethan wasn't sure what he was supposed to say. Felix unlaced his boots, and pushed them off, removing socks and unbuckling his belt.

"Five minutes." Felix chuckled this time, then gave

an accompanying shake of his head. He unbuttoned the jeans that fit him like a second skin and eased them down over his hips. Ethan got an eyeful of the shape of Felix's cock, clearly outlined in boxer briefs, and very interested in the thought of sex. Ethan squirmed a little. Of course, he'd imagined what it might be like to have Felix fucking him, but the reality and the chance of it happening wasn't something he'd considered.

Felix went into the bathroom, and Ethan heard some rummaging before Felix crossed to him and sunk gracefully to his knees in front of him.

"Sit back in the chair." Felix was firm, and in a smooth move, he removed the last layer, his soft, worn gray T-shirt. He was naked now, apart from the boxers, and he was right there on his knees in front of Ethan. A sudden thought hit Ethan that this was some kind of pity thing—that had happened to him before, and he'd always talked himself out of it. Maybe that was what he should do now? Explain with care how he didn't want to mess things up, so Felix should give up now, and that Felix didn't need to feel sorry for him. Still, that didn't stop Ethan from moving back in the chair until he was settled, and when Felix placed his hands on the arms, Ethan was trapped.

"I'm going to help you with this belt," Felix murmured, undid that and unbuttoned Ethan's jeans, and then nodded. "Lift."

Ethan did as he was told, his head buzzing with reasons this shouldn't be happening, his mouth dry, and his chest still tight. Felix eased the denim down, removing Ethan's socks, and then, in a smooth move, his jeans.

"Okay, now the shirt. Unbutton it. Take it off. And your T-shirt."

Something in Felix's tone left no room for discussion, and Ethan followed the instructions, the coolness of the room, despite the warm air, making his skin prickle. Felix stared into Ethan's eyes, and as he held the gaze, he pressed his hands flat to Ethan's chest.

"Five minutes would never be enough time for what I want to do with you," Felix said. He brushed Ethan's nipples, then squeezed them gently between his thumb and forefinger. "You have such pretty nipples," he whispered, rolling them.

In that instant, Ethan found out something very new about himself; it seemed he freaking loved having his nipples played with so much that he whined low in his throat and shifted his hips. The pinching sensations led straight to his cock. He was already hard, and all the words that'd normally have tumbled out stayed inside his head.

"Do you like them being sucked?" Felix asked.

With hindsight, Ethan knew he must have said something, although it had probably been gibberish, because he was desperate for Felix to suck him. He was humping the air as if that was going to help. Felix kissed his left nipple, his fingers still pressing and pulling at the right, and then he sucked the nub into his mouth and worried it, bit gently, and—holy fuck if Felix didn't stop, then Ethan was going to come way too soon.

"Felix, you need to…" Stop? Carry on? Talk to me? Ethan didn't know what he was asking for. "Harder."

Felix smiled, sucked harder, pulled, eased himself between Ethan's knees, getting him to spread his legs, until he rested on Ethan, his cock close to Ethan's. He needed pressure; he needed fingers on him and in him, and he moved to reach for himself.

Felix was there first, nudging his hands to one side. "Not yet," he said, and held Ethan's hands in one of his.

Ethan could've pulled them free if he wanted, but there was something about the way Felix was controlling this that meant Ethan could let himself go. It wasn't Ethan trying to guide any of this, it wasn't him demanding this or that. He was here for the ride. Felix kissed from nipple to throat, and then leaned up and pressed his lips against Ethan's. The kiss at first was gentle, and then Felix pressed his tongue to Ethan's, tangling, and tasting, and praising Ethan with kisses before they took a breath.

"You can touch my hair," Felix encouraged.

Ethan realized his hands were free, and he laced his fingers into Felix's soft hair. The kisses were deep, and Ethan wanted to hold Felix so close and kiss, only it seemed Felix had another idea. He broke the embrace, and even though Ethan chased for more, Felix was already heading south—a kiss and suck on each nipple, tracing a path to his navel, scooting backward a little, kissing Ethan's hipbone, his chin nudging Ethan's erection. "I want to taste this."

Was he asking for permission? What should Ethan be saying? He was confused. He had so much he wanted to ask for, so much he'd never experienced before, and he wanted it all with Felix.

"Suck me, please."

Felix eased down his boxers, pulling them over his knees and tossing them behind him. And throughout it all, Ethan didn't let go of his hair.

"I'm going to suck you," Felix murmured, "and I've got hotel lotion, and I'm going to put my fingers in you, pressing gently to loosen you up, but you can't come with me sucking. Wait until I'm inside you. Is that all okay?"

"Huh?"

"I need your words, Ethan. I want to get inside you. I need to loosen you. I want you to ride my fingers. I've got you. Is that okay?"

"Fuck, yes." Ethan had never heard anything so erotic in his life.

Felix licked Ethan's cock from root to tip and then again, tugging him forward and encouraging him to tilt his hips. The first touch of Felix's fingers to his hole corresponded with him sucking on the head of his cock. Then, he set a rhythm that involved taking Ethan's cock down his throat, then sucking his way up the length. Ethan wanted to touch and feel. He released his hold on Felix's hair, traced Felix's cheeks, which hollowed as he sucked.

He arched up into Felix's mouth. "I'm going to… I'm going… Felix…"

Felix stopped sucking, although his fingers were still pressed to Ethan's hole, and there was the slickness of lotion as Felix worked him open. Ethan was on the edge.

All he'd need was a little friction to his cock, and he'd come so damn hard. But Felix wasn't touching Ethan's neglected cock. Instead, he sat back on his heels as if he was concentrating hard on what he was doing. Then, he leaned down and sucked each ball. Ethan took advantage of twisting his fingers in Felix's hair, loving the texture of it, adoring how Felix was prepping him.

"Stand up," Felix said, and extended a hand to help Ethan. "Sit on the edge of the bed."

Felix wiped his fingers on tissues, then rooted in his discarded jeans. "Thank fuck," he muttered, and pulled out a condom, waving it in his hand. "Negative, PrEP, always use condoms, you?"

It took a moment for Ethan's thoughts to catch up with the sensible conversation. "All of that."

"Do you want to do this?"

Ethan widened his legs and smiled. "Yep."

Felix didn't hesitate. He rolled on the condom, then ran his hands to Ethan's knees and pushed him back. "Look at you, all spread out and sexy. I've watched you all day and wanted to kiss you. God, you're so beautiful."

"You make me feel…" Beautiful. In an instant, Ethan was shy.

"I'm going to try to make this last," Felix chuckled, "but your body…"

He pressed his cock against Ethan's hole and pushed gently. Ethan felt a sudden panic that he would fuck this up, or that he wouldn't know what to do. He wanted Felix inside; he wanted to be filled, and he *really* wanted to come, but did he have to ask or beg for more?

"Push down," Felix encouraged. "Let me in." Finally, Felix filled him, and stretched him, and leaned over to kiss him, as he bottomed out. He was giving Ethan time to relax, letting his body get used to the intrusion. The kisses were a tangle of tongues, accompanied by the sweetest words of praise and the most erotic sexy statements from Felix against Ethan's lips.

"So sexy, so deep. I want you so bad. You're so gorgeous. I want to fuck you hard, and make you come all over your beautiful, soft skin. I want you... I need you. So perfect..."

"Please..." Ethan moaned.

Finally, Felix moved, rocking into him, still kissing, capturing Ethan's hands, and holding them above his head. When his cock pressed Ethan's prostate, it was very close to being game over, but that was just the start. Felix rested a knee on the bed, and with the extra traction, he fucked him, each push accompanied by a deep and searching kiss. Trapped between them, Ethan's neglected cock was begging to be touched, but Felix didn't release his hands, and this high of desperation and need was the most stunning thing Ethan had ever experienced.

"I'm close," Felix murmured, and released one of Ethan's hands. "Touch yourself. I want to see you come."

Ethan was all too happy to comply, and it didn't take much more than a few tugs of his cock, and everything that'd been promised in Felix's kisses was blown away by the most intense orgasm. The room spun, his breathing was ragged, and he watched as, above him, Felix was lost in his own completion. He stared down at Ethan and captured one more kiss as he pushed hard and then, stilled deep inside, and cursed as he came, biting down on Ethan's neck, groaning his release.

They stayed joined in the awkward position for a few moments, and then Felix eased out, tied off the condom, and headed to the bathroom. When he came back, he brought a damp cloth and some cream, wiping his own belly, then Ethan's, before massaging more of the motel's cream around Ethan's hole, taking care of him.

I feel special. I feel… every good thing.

Ethan was boneless and tired, and he crab-walked back up the bed, Felix followed, and together they snuggled under the covers in complete silence. For the first time in days, weeks, years even, Ethan's thoughts were silent as he snuggled in Felix's arms.

"See?" Felix teased. "It's better if it lasts longer than five minutes."

All Ethan could do was agree, and he kissed that agreement onto Felix's skin. If this was the only sexy hotel only-one-bed experience he'd ever have—the best sex—then the apocalypse could happen now, and he'd die a happy man.

Chapter Thirteen

Where am I?

Felix stared at the unfamiliar ceiling. He blinked,
then lowered his gaze as he checked out the room he'd
woken in.

Ah, I remember.

Pain shot through his shoulder as he went to raise his
arm. With a grunt, he rolled his neck and found himself
staring at the top of Ethan's head. Ethan's hair brushed
against his cheek, and he smiled, remembering what had
happened between them last night.

Kisses, sex, cuddling.

They'd fallen asleep wrapped in a hug.

He winced as he tried to figure out how to free his
arm without disturbing Ethan. He looked so peaceful.

Whatever. He rested his chin on the top of Ethan's
head and listened to the sound of Ethan's breathing,
appreciating the warmth of Ethan's body. Maybe this
was worth sacrificing an arm.

"Are you awake?" Ethan mumbled against Felix's

chest. His words tickled a path across Felix's skin. He groaned as he stretched his arms out in front of him and squirmed.

"Yeah." Felix lifted his arm, encouraging Ethan to move. Ethan shuffled back to lie on his pillow. "Owie," Felix said with a chuckle and rubbed his shoulder.

"Are you okay?" Ethan stared up at him all doe-eyed with a soft expression, having just woken. He blinked slowly.

Felix nodded. "My arm's gone numb, that's all. Nothing serious." He shifted onto his side and grabbed his phone off the nightstand. They had about an hour until they needed to check out. "Do you want to shower first?" He smiled when Ethan hugged him and buried his head between his shoulder blades. "Tired?" he asked.

"A bit."

"You're okay though, right?" He glanced over his shoulder. "Not aching too much?"

Ethan snorted into his back.

Felix rolled over to face Ethan. He smiled and flattened Ethan's bed hair. "There, that's better." He leaned forward, pressing a kiss to Ethan's forehead before settling with his hand on Ethan's waist.

What am I supposed to say in this situation?

Last night had been amazing. Ethan had been amazing. Maybe too amazing as, right then, Felix was at a loss for words. Instead, he stared into Ethan's eyes, enjoying the warm glow they held.

Where do we go from here?

It was Ethan who looked away first as he dropped

his head forward. "It was good last night, wasn't it? Was I good?"

Felix repositioned his head on his pillow and tried to catch Ethan's eye. "What kind of question is that?"

"I just—" Felix shut him up with a kiss. "Oh."

"It's too early in the morning for you to be overthinking." Felix pulled Ethan by the waist, hugging him closer. "Besides, I'm pretty sure last night spoke for itself." He bumped his nose to Ethan's, wanted to blow away the lingering doubt in Ethan's eyes. "It was good. I had fun." He moved his mouth to Ethan's ear, nipping his earlobe, then said in a low voice, "And you were great." He smiled when Ethan squirmed.

"That tickles," Ethan said and covered his ear. He glanced down, hesitated for a moment before saying, "I had fun, too."

Felix pressed a kiss to Ethan's cheek. "I'm glad."

"I guess I should start saving now."

"Hmm?"

"To hire you for more dates."

Felix frowned. Was Ethan really going to ignore everything he said yesterday? "You do understand yesterday wasn't a booking, don't you?"

Ethan nodded. "I know. I remember you implied that, but…"

"But what?"

"I don't want today to be the last time I see you. I want to see you again, keep seeing you. I don't want this to be the only time we…" He traced Felix's shoulder and across his chest. "So, if the only way for that to happen is to hire you then—"

"I don't sleep with clients," Felix stated. He realized that he'd probably sounded a little too blunt.

"But last night we…"

With a sigh, Felix shifted until he could take hold of Ethan's face, a hand on each cheek. He squeezed so Ethan's lips formed a pout. "Is it really so hard to believe I visited your parents, spent time with you, slept with you because I *wanted* to?" He paused, taking a moment to study everything about Ethan—lips, eyes, his gaze, the way his nose was scrunched up in confusion. He stroked Ethan's cheeks with his thumbs.

Why did Ethan struggle to believe Felix was interested in him as more than a client? Did he think so little of Felix, of himself?

Felix considered his words. Ethan had blurted out his confession way back at his department Christmas party. Felix on the other hand…

I probably wouldn't believe me either.

He leaned forward and kissed Ethan. He hadn't wanted to rush a decision about returning Ethan's feelings. It had been easy to be drawn in. Ethan was fascinating, quirky, sweet, different from anyone Felix had gotten close to. He had wanted to take his time and sort through his feelings. Yesterday had helped a lot. He had been able to spend time with Ethan without the weight of it being a job, of fakeness and pretend. At least, it had been that way for him. Ethan kept bringing them, their *relationship* back to where they had started.

"Ethan," he said. He took a moment to flatten Ethan's bangs, then returned his hand to his face. "I like you." The words were heavy in his chest. It had been years since he had last said to someone like or love, and confessed attraction. He looked into Ethan's eyes, relished the connection they had, and was sure he wanted only to deepen it.

"You like me?" Ethan's brow creased as he raised his eyebrows.

"Yes," he said on a chuckle. "Last night didn't clue you in?"

Ethan broke eye contact. "I didn't want to assume."

"I thought you said you remembered what I told you before we got to your folks' place?"

"I do. It's just difficult."

"What is?"

"Hearing that kind of stuff."

Felix stroked Ethan's cheek. "Why?"

Ethan shook his head. "I don't know. It's how I am. I overthink things, and I don't want to get my hopes up only to be brought down with a huge bump." He huffed. "I mean, look at me. Why would anyone—"

Felix tapped Ethan's lips with his thumb, then pressed to keep him silent. Was it down to another open door that Ethan really couldn't see himself as worth something more than a short-lived fling, or sex and done?

"Let's date," he said. "We should date."

Ethan swallowed and worried his bottom lip.

Felix pecked a kiss to the corner of Ethan's mouth. "Well?"

Another peck to his chin.

Ethan squirmed.

Felix kissed him again. "Just say *yes* already." He leaned in again, only for Ethan to break free.

"Okay, okay. You can stop." Embarrassment colored Ethan's face. "Yes."

With a smile, Felix dragged Ethan back into a tight hug, their stomachs pressing together as he nuzzled Ethan's neck.

"Happy now?" Ethan asked.

Felix lifted his head and nodded. He was the happiest he'd been in a long time.

The journey home was slow, but it was more to do with the random snowfall than lines of traffic, and all too soon Felix was parked and after a quick kiss, Ethan climbed out of the car

"I'll call you, okay?" Felix called after him.

Ethan bent down and looked through the open passenger side window. "Okay." He hesitated.

"What's wrong?" Felix said softly.

Ethan shook his head. "Nothing. I just… Thanks for yesterday."

With a smile, Felix said, "My pleasure. It was lovely meeting your family. Next time, maybe you can come with me to see my mom and dad."

"Your mom and dad?" Ethan said with wide eyes. "Really?"

"Of course. You have no idea how happy it'd make Mom."

Ethan's expression brightened. "I'd like that."

"Okay. I'll let you get inside. Don't want you catching a cold." He chuckled. "I'll be in touch soon."

"Sure." Ethan stepped back from the car and raised his hand. "Bye."

After returning Ethan's wave, Felix closed the window, then pulled away.

As he drove his mind was full of Ethan and what came next. He wanted them to spend more time together, just the two of them.

I hope it can happen soon.

Work was busy, and Christmas was right around the corner.

I'll figure something out.

Once he made it home, he showered, changed into sweatpants and a hoodie, and settled on the couch. "So tired," he groaned and raised his shoulders. With a sigh, he stared at the 3D puzzles on the coffee table. He hadn't found the time to solve either of them.

He picked up the pieces of the dismantled cross and rested them in his lap. He imagined Ethan would be able to put them together easily.

Or would he?

Being book smart didn't seem as if it would be all that useful.

Fishing his cell phone from his pocket, Felix rang his mom. When she answered, he put her on speaker and lay his phone on the cushion beside him.

"Hello," she said. "Are you home?"

Felix examined some of the pieces as he talked. "Yes. I got back maybe thirty minutes ago. Wanted to wash up first." He held two of the pieces together as he tried to fit the others around them. "I'll probably eat, then bring the car back. Is there anything you want me to pick up on the way? I can stop by the store. Food or...?"

"I can't think of anything. Just bring yourself and the car."

"Will do." He slotted another piece and, suddenly, felt hopeful about the space remaining to fit the others into.

"Did you have fun?"

"Hmm?"

"It wasn't work, was it? You said it was a favor for a friend?" There was a hint of curiosity in her voice.

Felix held the pieces together as he considered what to say. "No, it wasn't work." Should he say more? "And yes, I had fun." He smiled as he remembered.

"Who did you say you were with? I forget."

Felix laughed. "Nice try, but I don't think I told you anything aside from him being a friend."

"You're so much like your father it's annoying. You're no fun at all, either of you."

Felix twisted the puzzle, surprised when he managed to fit in the last pieces. "His name's Ethan," he said and admired the completed cross.

"Ethan. And Ethan is just a," she paused, "*friend?*"

He held the 3D cross. It was strange how, sometimes, things worked out, came together, and just fit. "I don't know." He eyed his cell phone. Whatever he would label Ethan as, it was no longer simply as *friend*. "We're not together, together. But I asked him out, and he said yes."

Though they hadn't arranged anything official yet, he was confident in saying, "We're dating."

It seemed his mom was lost for words, as she remained silent.

"Are you that shocked?" He swapped the puzzle for his cell phone, turned off the speaker and held his phone to his ear.

"Honestly, a little bit." She laughed. "Do we get to meet him?"

Felix sucked on his teeth. "I don't know. Maybe." Meeting Felix's parents would probably help put Ethan's mind at ease, know that Felix was serious about him. "Maybe after Christmas? I still have work, and I don't know what his plans will be for the holidays."

"Wait," his mom said. "Are you feeling all right? Did you really just agree to us meeting him?" He could almost hear the dumb smile she must have been wearing.

"All right, all right. Do you want me to change my mind?"

"No, no. I won't tease you anymore. I was just surprised. It's been a long time since you brought someone over."

Felix shuffled to lay on the couch. "It's been a long time since I've had anyone to bring." He stared at the ceiling, a smile curling his lips as he thought about Ethan.

I have a good feeling this time, about things working out, about him.

"You can interrogate me more later when I bring the car over. I'm going to go make a sandwich."

"Sounds good. See you later, baby."

"Bye."

Felix stared at his phone after he hung up. Was it too soon to contact Ethan? He wanted to see him.

He sent a message to Ethan because he at least wanted to put the idea out there.

Let's get coffee soon.

Chapter Fourteen

Coffee didn't happen the next day, or the day after, although Felix messaged at odd moments—about the snow, or Christmas, or Jared, or how much he was looking forward to a next date. Ethan couldn't help but think that Felix was very busy proving he wanted to date Ethan, but between their chat and the kissing, Ethan had already worked that out for himself. Which was handy, given that all Ethan wanted to do was date Felix.

He loved receiving every single message, but they always appeared when he was busy, or when his thought process was taken up with chemicals and equations. He always meant to get back to them, assumed that Felix would understand why he wasn't responding, then worried that Felix wouldn't understand at all. Which was why he was pacing his small apartment and fretting about how to be a boyfriend.

"I'm not very good at this," he announced to Jared, who was studying. "Jared? I'm not very good at this," he said louder, forcing Jared to glance up from his books, blinking.

"Huh?" Jared reached for the coffee at his side, sipping it and wrinkling his nose in distaste. "How did it get so cold?"

"It's the thermic process——"

"Rhetorical question, Einstein." He placed the mug back on the table and stretched. "Wassup?"

"Felix is messaging me. Sending me pictures of *things*."

Jared raised an eyebrow. "*Things*? What kinds of *things*? Actually, don't answer that. I don't want to know."

"Look at this." Ethan shoved his phone under Jared's nose, and Jared covered his eyes.

"Shit. Is it his junk? I genuinely don't want to look at Felix's junk right now."

"No, it's a cat wearing a reindeer hat. Look!"

"If that's a euphemism for Felix with antlers on his cock, I will kill you." Jared opened his eyes and peered at the card. "Aww, that's kinda cute."

"I don't know what to do with it," Ethan said. "I mean, do I need to find an animal wearing a Santa hat to send back to him? I tried to find one, but there is a joke with his; read it."

Jared took the card with its sad cat wearing knitted antlers front and center. "So, the cat is saying; 'what do you mean Santa has enough reindeer?'" He chuckled. "Yeah, I can see the joke with the cat's sad eyes." He glanced up at Ethan who stared back, because he *really* needed Jared to be specific with his advice. "It's funny."

"Is it really though? Because the only other picture I found was of a puppy, and there was no joke. It was just a puppy in a Santa hat." He blew out a breath. "Should I send him something with a joke? It's all so confusing."

"Sit down," Jared said and pointed at the chair opposite him. Ethan took the seat and shuffled to face his friend, waiting for the wisdom to be given. "You're overthinking this, and you only overthink things when your brain is already going a million miles an hour. So, what's up?"

"Nothing, work is good; however, a whole new set of results came in, which is interesting because—"

"Okay, so work is good," Jared summarized quickly. "Are you worried about this thing with Felix? He's one of the good guys, you know."

There was so much to tell Jared, from taking Felix home to meet his family, to stopping at the motel on the way back, to possibly the most erotic experience he'd ever had, to the fact that now he and Felix had slid into some kind of relationship that involved sending each other cute pictures. They were dating, right? But was it actually a relationship? What even *was* a relationship? They hadn't managed coffee yet, but every time Felix messaged him, Ethan was knocked sideways by the force of the feelings inside him.

So how to sum all that up? "Yesterday, I was running a timed experiment, working within the properties of… You don't need to know that. Anyway, my phone vibrated, and I actually looked at it. Just to see if it was from Felix. And it was. It was that cat wearing the antlers, and it made me smile, and Daniel wanted to know what was so funny about single and double replacement, and I had to explain to him that there was nothing funny about single and double replacement, and he did this weird face thing." Ethan gestured to his own face and frowned. "So, I stopped talking about the photo and went back to my experiment. But I really love it that Felix is sending me these things, and I'm sending things back, and I really want to have coffee with him. So actually, I think we're dating, and the Felix thing is going okay, in its own way."

Jared smiled. "That's good news. So, if it's not work, and it's not Felix, then what else is making your mind run a million miles an hour?"

Ethan rested his chin on his fists and stared at his friend. "Open doors. Marcus at prom. I can't figure things out, and I think I'm supposed to be figuring it out. Like, when Marcus came into the bathroom, and it was just him and me, he seemed softer, as if he wanted to say something to me. But that all changed when Zed and Johnny barreled in after him, and I saw something in his expression that I just can't forget. I just don't know what it was."

Jared reached for Ethan's phone, and typed out a quick message, pressing send before Ethan could even ask what he was typing.

"What did you send?" Ethan asked. "Was it the puppy thing? The one without a joke?"

Before Jared could answer, Ethan's phone lit up with a reply, and Jared turn the phone so Ethan could read.

The message that Jared had sent was to Felix and

was to the point: *Want to meet up and drive to fix something?*
xx

The answer was sweet and direct. *Fix something?*
Sounds ominous. Sure. Pick you up in thirty? I'll bring coffee. xx

There were returned *xxs*. Ethan felt all warm inside,
then it hit him what Jared had done.

"Wait, I told you that Felix and I are okay. You don't
need to arrange dates for me. I know I'm not answering
his messages as much as I should, but he knows—"

Jared leaned over and flicked Ethan's forehead. "Get
Felix to drive you to wherever Marcus works or lives, talk
to the guy, and close the door, then you can let your big
brain cool down. Also, drink coffee with Felix, and talk
to him, and maybe enjoy that, for the first time, you're
more interested in someone, rather than chemical
equations."

Ethan waited as Jared scrolled through Google using
the limited information they had and then, armed with
the fact that Marcus appeared to be a partner in a car
service company, he grabbed his coat, wallet, and keys,
and took the stairs to the lobby. He burst out into the
cold air, straight into Felix's arms, kissing him soundly
and hugging him close. Felix kissed him back, cradling
his face, and easing him away before hauling him in and
kissing him again.

"I might not send as many messages as you do, but I
missed you."

"I missed you, too," Felix said.

"That's never happened to me before. Missing
someone I'm dating, I mean. And we are sending cute
animals to each other, and Jared says—"

Felix stopped him with another kiss. "Yes, we're dating. We've had that conversation already, and as much as I'd love to stand here kissing you all day, I left my car in a no-parking zone, so we really need to move. Dad will kill me if I get a ticket, or worse, get towed." Ethan followed Felix to the car, the scent of coffee filling the interior, and when they were buckled in, Felix gestured to the road in front of them. "Where to?"

"Oh, hang on. Lester's garage: I have the Code." He read out the details as Felix entered the information into his phone to use the GPS.

"Near where the reunion was?"

"Yeah." Ethan was lost in thought, and Felix didn't press for more, turning up the music and humming along with the Christmas songs blitzing the airwaves. They headed out of the city, and the closer they got to their destination, the more tense Ethan became. Felix was chatting about last night's date—a visiting executive who was trying to impress some new investors, but who drank way too much and ended up spending a long time in the bathroom being sick.

"… So, I'm there, holding his hair back. One investor comes into the bathroom, he was this Texas guy, and was super impressed that my date had drunk most of the table dry. They did the deal, right there in the bathroom."

"Huh?" Ethan picked up on that last part and wrinkled his nose. "Was that even sanitary?"

"Only you could think of that," Felix teased.

"Well, when you think of what kinds of bacteria can be found in most bathrooms—"

"No! Don't tell me or I'll never use public bathrooms again." Felix laughed.

Ethan loved that he could make Felix laugh. It was as if he'd found some hidden superpower, and he wisely decided not to mention that the same bacteria lived at home. The journey didn't take long, and all too soon, Felix had parked outside Lester's garage. It wasn't the most salubrious of places—a little rundown—but it looked honest with its faded sign and pile of used tires outside, as if people had worked here for many generations. There were two gas pumps and the small parking area where Felix had stopped.

"So, you want to tell me why we are here? As much as I love drinking coffee outside random garages, I'm thinking something more important is going on, given how serious you look."

Ethan faced Felix and sighed. "Marcus works here."

Felix's smile dropped, and he was cautious. "And we're here because…?"

"There was something about what happened. When he first came into the bathroom, he was nervous, scared even. He only got all funny when the other two came in. I just need to know what happened, and whether… I don't know. I'm probably not making any sense."

"Can I come in with you? I'd like to; if that's okay?" Felix's expression was serious and focused, but he couldn't know how much Ethan needed him to go in with him. Somehow he'd become as important a part of Ethan as Jared was, more important even.

"That's exactly what I want. He might not even be working today, but maybe they can contact him for me, or something? Jared says he has a Facebook that hasn't been used in a few years, so I can't rely on that being much use. Who knows if he checks it and it's not like I use social media, and even if he saw my message he might not reply." Ethan subsided as Felix laid a hand on his knee, squeezing it.

"Let's go in and see." He killed the engine, and they headed toward the door marked reception. Only they didn't have to go inside at all. The main door opened, and Marcus stepped through, carrying a large box. He stopped abruptly. He wore a huge puffy coat with *Lester's Garage* embroidered on the chest, and there was a smudge of oil on his cheek. He was still the big man Ethan remembered, broad, square-jawed, and a little soft around the edges. Ethan didn't know what to say next.

"What do you want?" Marcus demanded, his brow furrowing as he glanced at a very tense and watchful Felix. "I don't want any trouble."

"We're not here to cause trouble," Ethan reassured him. "I just wanted to talk."

"Fuck. Okay." Marcus went from defensive to resigned in a split second. "Wait here." He placed the box on top of the two already there, steadying them so they were balanced, and then disappeared back into reception. Felix laced his fingers with Ethan's and held tight, offering reassurance even though Ethan didn't feel as if he needed it right now. He'd seen that moment of resignation, and there was something else in Marcus that he couldn't work out. Sadness? Maybe Marcus had his own open doors to deal with.

He came back out, gesturing for them to follow him around the back of the garage to where a wooden trestle table with benches sat just inside a shelter. Marcus had added a woolly hat and a long scarf in deference to the icy weather, and he looked more like an innocent teddy bear than the ghost who might haunt Ethan's fears.

"I don't want people knowing I'm talking to you." Marcus was back on the defensive, sitting on the far end of the bench as if he was putting as much distance between him and Ethan as he could. "They might get the wrong idea."

"About what?" Ethan asked.

"About you being gay and all, and me… well, I'm not." He stopped talking as if he'd run out of words.

Ethan glanced at Felix, who squeezed his hand. "I want you to explain what happened in the bathroom back at prom."

Marcus tilted his chin. "Fuck's sake. I'm sorry, okay? This is me apologizing. Are we done?" He went to leave, but Ethan stopped him with a question.

"Please, tell me what *really* happened."

"What *really* happened?" Marcus sounded incredulous. "I tried to kiss you; it was too much. That's exactly how it went down."

"So, you grabbed me, shoved me against the counter, and then forced a kiss on me. That's what a police report would say, right?" Ethan got the feeling he was pushing things to the limit when Marcus went pale before tilting his chin again, his eyes flaring.

"You want to go to the police? Then do it. I'll just plead guilty to being drunk and stupid and tell them I thought it was mutual." Guilt slid over his face, and he couldn't meet Ethan's steady gaze.

Felix bristled. "You know damn well it wasn't Ethan—"

"It's okay, Felix, I've got this," Ethan reassured him, and for the first time, he felt as if he *did* have this. "I'm guessing your story won't change because you don't want anybody from school thinking that you might have wanted to kiss me to start with. Your story won't change because you don't want anybody knowing that you were queer? People like Zed and Johnny?"

"I'm not fucking queer!" he exclaimed.

"I think you might be," Ethan murmured.

Marcus's mouth fell open, and he stared at Ethan and then, down at the table. He was fighting something hard, and a sob caught in his throat; when he glanced up again, his expression was tortured.

"You were the lucky one—you got to go to college, you got to leave town, you got to make yourself out to be whatever you wanted. Some of us had to stay." His eyes swam with tears. "I liked you more than you know. I used to watch you sometimes, so sweet and confusing, and I had all these feelings that didn't belong. At least, not to the captain of the football team. It was..." The tears spilled down his cheeks, and he wiped at them, staring at his hands as if he couldn't believe they were wet. "I tried to kiss you, but I was clumsy and stupid, and then the guys came in, but I didn't mean to hurt you... I just wanted to be different with you that night, only I couldn't be. I can't be different. I'm trapped, and everything I feel is a secret. I can't even tell Neil how I really feel."

Ethan wasn't sure who Neil was—it wasn't a name he remembered from the reunion, but his heart hurt from hearing Marcus's story. What must it be like to be stuck in the persona of who you were in school? Locked into a cycle of expectation, feeling as if the only validation you deserved was from who you were pretending to be ten years ago.

"I scared people. I didn't fit in my skin," Marcus mumbled, and wiped away the last of his tears, straightening his shoulders, refusing to allow vulnerability to take hold. "I'm not that person anymore, but everyone expects—"

"Marcus! You out here?" A short man came around the corner, his copper-red hair standing out against his rainbow jacket. The new guy stopped and smiled. "Hi." He shook hands with Felix and then, Ethan. "Neil, Marcus's business partner. Are you here for the Corvette? We weren't expecting you for another hour, but it's ready to go—"

"They're not here for the Corvette, Neil. Please, just give me five minutes with them," Marcus interrupted.

Neil frowned, then touched Marcus on the shoulder. "All right, big guy. As long as you're okay. Yeah?"

"I'm okay."

"See you inside." He smiled down at Marcus with affection, then sauntered back toward the main building.

"I said I was sorry, and I genuinely mean it," Marcus offered as soon as Neil was out of hearing range. "But I don't know what else to say to you. If the cops come..."

he closed his eyes for a moment, "I'll tell them what really happened. I'll tell Zed and Johnny. Fuck them both. I'm so sorry."

"We're not getting the cops involved in anything. All I need for you to do is promise me that, when you're ready, you tell Neil how you feel, get some counseling, and close some doors."

"I don't get it. What doors?"

"You'll see. But also, take my number, message me if you need to talk."

"You don't need me anywhere near you."

"We all need friends," Ethan said. He didn't have a pen, nor any idea how to pass over his number through the phone, but Felix had his back. He took Ethan's phone, found a number, and held it up to Marcus. At first, Marcus did nothing except stare, and then he swallowed, his eyes bright with emotion again.

After a pause he took out his own phone and added Ethan's number, sending a brief message to check. Then, he stood and extended a hand to Ethan.

"You're a better man than me," he murmured.

"I don't know about that, but I get the feeling that, if you were honest with Neil… Well, I wish you luck with Neil." Ethan felt lighter, as if he'd dispatched one more ghost and maybe—finally—shut that door on his experience at school. Now, all he needed to focus on was being the best boyfriend to Felix, and not scaring him away.

"Are you okay?" Felix asked when they were back in the car.

He leaned over and pressed a soft kiss to Felix's lips.

"More than okay. You know, I think I could love you," he added, and his chest tightened. He hadn't meant to let that slip out. Was it too soon? Was it Christmas magic working its way into their lives?

"Me too," Felix said after a pause. "It's very easy to think I could love you."

Life was good.

Chapter Fifteen

Finally, a proper coffee date.

Felix sat back and watched Ethan devour a slab of chocolate cake. The dainty eater he thought he was familiar with from the few times food had been involved when they were together was gone. It seemed that cake brought out a wild, hungry side.

"Is it good?" he asked.

Ethan lowered his fork and licked his lips. Clearing his throat, he nodded. "Did you want some?" The lack of eye contact and the way he held the plate close to his chest gave Felix the impression that Ethan, in no way, wanted to share.

Felix chuckled. "I'm fine. I might grab a slice of their cherry pie later." For the time being, he was happy with his mocha. He eyed his drink and the melting whipped cream.

"Okay." Ethan looked relieved as he picked up his fork and continued eating.

Was now a good time to ask?

Leaning forward, Felix ran his finger down the side of his mug. "What are you doing Christmas Day? Or more specifically in the afternoon?"

"Me?" Ethan covered his mouth and swallowed. "Um, I don't know. Jared will be with Nate and Luka, and I was invited, but I don't think I want to intrude, so, TV and snacks." He smiled.

"You don't spend it with any of your family?"

Ethan shook his head. "With Mom and Dad out of town, us kids usually do our own thing. Sean has the girls, so they do their own family thing, and Claire...it depends. Last year, she went to a ski resort with friends. I can't remember if she said what she was doing this time." He wiped at the corner of his mouth. "Why?"

"I was wondering if you'd like to spend it with me and, maybe, meet my mom and dad," he said.

Since confronting Marcus, Ethan had changed a little. Maybe not *changed*, but rather, Felix felt as if Ethan had relaxed, accepted Felix was sticking around.

Ethan's eyes widened. "Meet your parents? Really?"

"Well, it seems only fair. I've met yours, after all." He picked up his drink, took a sip. "I had thought in the New Year, but..." Their relationship had been picking up speed, from messages to late night phone calls to, at last, a coffee date. "I want them to meet you. To meet my boyfriend."

"Oh." Ethan lowered his plate. "Okay. Yes. What do I do though? Should I bring them something?"

"Like what?"

"I don't know. A gift? To say thanks for making... you." He tilted his head. "Or not."

Felix laughed. "Definitely not. You don't need to bring anything, just yourself and your smile is enough."

"Really?"

"Really."

Ethan narrowed his eyes. "But I want to make a good impression. This is my first time meeting the parents of someone I'm dating. Well, actually, there was one time, but that was more by accident. We happened to bump into them on the street." He sighed, pouted. "I got dumped two days later."

What am I supposed to say to that?

"Erm, right. But seriously, you don't need to bring anything." Ethan stared at him. "Fine. How about some flowers for Mom and a bottle of red wine for my dad. But nothing expensive or fancy," he added.

Ethan's expression brightened as he smiled. "I can do that."

Warmth spread through Felix's chest. He hoped it would always be this easy to make Ethan smile.

I love it when he does.

I think I love him for everything he does.

Ethan arrived at Felix's mom and dad's place just after three in the afternoon, and Felix had already missed him more than he thought possible as he'd done the normal Christmas Day things with his family. *Maybe I should have asked him to come for the whole day.*

"Ethan." Felix rested his hands on Ethan's shoulders as he stood behind him. "Meet Mom and Dad."

Ethan straightened. "Hello. Nice to meet you."

So stiff.

Felix gently squeezed Ethan's shoulders, kneading his muscles. "Mom, Dad. This is Ethan." He wrapped his arm around Ethan's shoulders, hugging him from the back. "My boyfriend," he added.

His mom smiled. "Lovely to meet you. Karin," she pressed her hand to her chest, "and Charlie." She waved a hand over her shoulder to where Felix's dad was standing.

"Hi. Hi." Ethan held out the potted mini rose and bottle of wine he had brought as gifts.

"Oh, thank you. You didn't need to. But thank you." She took them and passed them up to her husband.

"You found us okay?" she said with a smile. "I told Felix he should come get you."

Felix huffed, "Maybe if you hadn't made me eat so much at lunch, I'd have managed to drag myself off the couch."

His mom shook her head. "Or rather if your father hadn't talked you into drinking with him."

"It was one beer," his dad uttered, then headed for the kitchen with the plant and wine.

"Two," she called after him.

There was an awkward pause.

"Well, come in, come in." She turned her chair, encouraging Ethan to follow her. Charlie left the kitchen to accompany her to the living room, having swapped Ethan's presents for another beer.

When there was a little distance between him and Felix's parents, Ethan relaxed his shoulders. He looked up at Felix.

"Okay?" Felix mouthed, rubbing his arm in support.

Ethan nodded.

Felix leaned his head to Ethan's and pressed a kiss to his cheek. "See. That wasn't difficult at all."

Huffing a breath, Ethan elbowed Felix in the stomach. "It's been like three minutes. There's still plenty of time for me to make a complete idiot of myself. What if they hate me? What if I can't stop myself from shooting off at a tangent from the conversation? What if—" Felix bopped him on the forehead. "What was that for?" He pouted.

"As I said, I'm full of lunch, and may have had a beer or two, so you're going to have to make me a promise today."

"A promise?" Ethan's cheeks puffed out as he thought over Felix's request.

"Yes. So, do you promise?"

"Aren't you going to tell me what it is first?" He quirked an eyebrow.

Felix rested his chin on Ethan's shoulder. "Nope. Just hurry up and promise so I can crash on the couch and cuddle up to my boyfriend."

After a pause, Ethan nodded. "Okay. I promise."

"Good."

"What did I just agree to?"

"You're not allowed to overthink for the rest of the afternoon." He ruffled Ethan's hair. "Okay?"

Ethan lowered his gaze but agreed. "Okay."

"Are you two planning on joining us or what?" Karin called from the living room.

"Coming," Felix shouted back. He pecked Ethan's cheek. "Come on."

To Felix's relief the time together with Ethan and his parents passed quickly. The atmosphere was comfortable, conversation flowed, and he was happy to see Ethan smile once again.

"Here, use this." He laughed as he wrapped a scarf around Ethan, playfully covering his whole face.

"Stop it," Ethan scolded and pulled the navy-blue woolen scarf down to sit beneath his chin.

"Some gloves, too." Felix handed them to Ethan.

Ethan took them and pulled them on. "Where are we going exactly?"

"For a walk. I need some fresh air before I fall asleep. Besides," he hugged Ethan to him. "I want some Ethan time."

A smile spread across Ethan's flushed face. "I suppose that's okay then." He relaxed into the hug.

Felix kissed him on the forehead, then released him. "So, I thought a romantic walk in the snow might be a nice way to get it." He fastened his coat, then held out his hand. "Shall we?"

When Ethan took his hand, Felix's heart swelled. He was glad Ethan was here.

"Back in a bit," he called to his parents and opened the front door.

Hand-in-hand, he and Ethan stepped out onto the fresh snow. It was quiet and there didn't seem to be anyone else around. The afternoon light was fading, the low sun casting a beautiful glow over the neighborhood.

Felix kept hold of Ethan's hand, pulling him to his

side as they walked together. The snow added a magical feel to the world around them, and Felix was warmed knowing he was sharing the moment with Ethan.

Who'd have thought Jared's request for a favor would have brought him and Ethan to this point?

"Happy?" Felix said, swinging his and Ethan's arms.

Ethan gripped his hand tightly. "Definitely."

They slipped into a comfortable silence as they made their way along the street. Some of the houses they passed had snowmen in front of them. The snow nearby had been kicked up and displaced. Other houses were illuminated by strings of Christmas lights and other flashing decorations. As night crept in, the fading sunlight meant they were bright and beautiful.

"This way," Felix said as they reached a small park. He'd used to play there as a kid.

There were fading footprints on the ground, the recent snow having almost erased them and returned the park to a perfect blanket of untouched white.

Felix let go of Ethan's hand and went over to the pair of swings. He brushed the seats clean and invited Ethan to sit down with him.

"Seriously?"

Felix sat first but flinched when he could feel the cold seat through his jeans. "Mmm," he managed, but Ethan saw through him.

"Cold by any chance?" Ethan folded his arms and stared at him through narrowed eyes.

"Maybe a little." Felix fidgeted as he held onto the chains.

Ethan laughed. "Not as romantic as you thought, huh?"

With a sigh, Felix stood and wiped his ass. "At least I tried."

"Yes. You did." Ethan stepped up to him and cupped his face. He stared at Felix, smiled, then drew him close and into a kiss.

Felix closed his eyes and shut out the world to focus only on the feel of Ethan's lips on his. He leaned into the kiss, pushing back.

Ethan pulled away, and Felix opened his eyes and stared at Ethan, and it hit him.

I think I love him.

He covered Ethan's hands, squeezed them, and went in for another kiss. Ethan's nose was cold as it nudged his own, and he tilted his head, parting his lips as their mouths met once more.

The kiss was firm, warm, everything. He moved his hands to Ethan's waist, guiding him forward, closer. He didn't want the moment to end, but eventually they parted, a soft sigh falling from Ethan's lips.

Their gazes met. Felix couldn't help himself and every feeling he had about Ethan spilled out in three words.

"I love you."

Ethan's eyes widened as they shone with surprise. "What?" he said, his voice almost a whisper.

The words Felix formed then came out as nothing but silence. He hesitated before finding the courage to say again, "I love you."

Ethan lowered his hands but held Felix's gaze. "Say it again."

Felix swallowed, glancing away for a moment, then repeated, "I love you."

"Wow." Ethan blinked and took a step back.

Regret tightened Felix's chest. *Did I make a mistake?*

"You don't have to say it back—"

"Shh." Ethan covered Felix's mouth. "Don't you dare ruin it."

Ruin it? Felix raised his eyebrows.

Ethan took a deep breath, then blurted, "I love you, too."

He does? Felix pulled Ethan's hand from his mouth, held on to him. They stared at each other, and they were both grinning like insane idiots.

"So, now what?" Ethan said. He straightened his back and checked around as if something was supposed to have changed in that moment.

Felix laughed. "What would you want to happen?"

"Fireworks? Flash mob? Hmm." Ethan tapped his chin. "Maybe…" He moved forward and surprised Felix with a clumsy peck to the lips.

Felix gripped Ethan by the wrist, dragging him close. He returned the kiss, one after another of playful pecks, until Ethan was chuckling and pushing him away. When they parted, Felix lifted his gaze. His cheek twitched as snowflakes fluttered above them, some landing on his face.

"It's snowing," Ethan stated.

"You're so smart."

Ethan gave him a light punch in the arm. "Be nice."

"Or what?" Felix smirked and raised an eyebrow.

"You're so…" Ethan bit his lip. "Naughty." He brushed his bangs, disturbing the snow that had started to collect in his hair. "Shall we go back?" He held out his hand.

With a nod, Felix laced his fingers with Ethan. "Sure."

As they walked, Ethan asked, "What are you doing tonight?"

Felix swung their arms. "I don't know. Home, I guess, unless I get a better offer." He turned his head, noted the way Ethan buried his chin in the scarf he was wearing.

Was it the cold or something else causing the flush of color in his cheeks?

"Will you stay with me?" Ethan said. "Stay over?"

Felix bumped his shoulder to Ethan's. "Of course." He leaned into Ethan, rested his head on Ethan's shoulder as they walked back in the snow. From now on, he would stay as often and as long as Ethan wanted him to.

He added, "You only had to ask."

Epilogue

One year later

"Everyone will be here in a minute," Felix announced from the door. Ethan wasn't sure why he'd thought it was a good idea to rearrange the kitchen cupboards at the last minute, but if Jared were here right now, he'd probably say something meaningful about the way Ethan was dealing with his nerves. Not that Ethan felt nervous, maybe over-excited, but whatever caused it, right now it was vitally important that Felix's and his rented place was tidy, with everything in order.

They'd only been living here for a few months—after the leases on both Ethan's and Felix's places were up, and a short period of sharing Felix's place—and it wasn't a showpiece of apartment living, but it was home for them for as long as they needed. It was theirs.

"I know exactly when everyone will be here. Jared has been giving me ten-minute warnings, for the last hour. Not to mention Marcus, who keeps messaging me with questions about what to bring. I told him we didn't need anything, but he and Neil are determined."

"And we're sure that asking Marcus and Neil to the party was the right idea? You don't think they'll be overwhelmed by our friends?" Felix took a container of dried fennel from Ethan's grasp and placed it between the cardamon and the jalapeno chili powder.

"It's a bit late to refuse them entry now that they're nearly here," Ethan began after some thought. "Anyway, Marcus is a friend—my friend at least."

Felix had found it hard to forgive as easily as Ethan had, but then he was overprotective in the best way.

"Yeah, I like the guy," Felix admitted grudgingly.

"He's a good guy now he's out and with Neil, plus Neil is a good fit for him, and… yeah… I think they can handle our friends." He picked up a pot of hot paprika and stared at the label. He'd barely been able to reach the dill so getting as far up as the Ps reminded him how little he'd thought this last-minute reordering through. "I'm just worried that everyone will get here expecting this really cute place, with me miraculously being the perfect host, when actually I'm so nervous that I accidentally mixed oregano into the Bs."

"We *do* have a really cute place," Felix said, removing the paprika from Ethan's precarious hold. The apartment had a living-dining room, one bedroom, and a shower room—the most they could afford to rent even in the cheaper parts of the city near where Ethan worked, but it was big enough for a few close friends to gather for drinks and pizza before heading over to

Rhea's where any of the boyfriends-for-hire who weren't working would be meeting up on Gideon's dime.

They were here a few more months anyway, then moving in the New Year to a small house in a quiet suburb outside Boston. Ethan had been lucky enough to have won a prestigious award for his work, and as a consequence, had had the pick of job offers from various universities. He and Felix had sat down and written a pros and cons list, and when they realized that what was important to them was family, they chose MIT, which was close to Ethan's family, and accommodated Felix's mother's wish to see him follow what, and who, he wanted. Felix's dad had healed, his mom had taken a few shaky steps out of her chair on one of the hottest days of the summer, and they were the first to encourage Felix to move on, pointing out, Boston wasn't the other side of the world.

That meant leaving New York and making a new start in a place where they were able to afford to buy property. Maybe get a dog, or start a family? Ethan was certain of his future with Felix, and wanted to suggest, with caution, that they get married, but he didn't want to mess it up. He couldn't decide between the ocean, or candlelight, swelling music, a stunning sunset, in the snow, loud or silent... Yeah, he had no idea how he would propose, but he had the ring; he just needed to find the perfect moment. Maybe it was now? Maybe it was right here in this shabby kitchen in a temporary apartment where he'd had the happiest year of his life loving Felix.

"We don't *really* have a cute place," Ethan said

instead, and offered a rueful smile as he waved at the beige walls and the faded drapes.

"Any place that has you in it is cute." Felix pressed a kiss to the end of his nose, and then, in one smooth move, lifted Ethan onto the counter and spread his legs to settle between them.

"You're so nice to me," Ethan said.

"That part is easy because I love you."

"I love you too. I don't know what I'd do without you."

Felix smiled into the next kiss. "You have that backward. It's more like what would I do without *you*?"

"Well, for a start you'd have to organize all your own spices and herbs," Ethan deadpanned.

They kissed some more, Ethan linking his fingers behind Felix's head, and regretting that he had to let go when Felix eased himself away and turned serious. For a brief moment, Ethan wondered if the spice and herb thing was a deal breaker, but that was stupid. Felix had seen him at his most confused and closed off, and like Jared, Felix went with the flow. There was no one more perfect for Ethan, than Felix.

"I can't imagine my life without you being part of it," Felix said, his eyes shining with emotion.

"Same," Ethan whispered. "Forever." Now was definitely the right time for him to propose—he could feel it in his heart, and the words were on the tip of his tongue as tears pricked his eyes.

Felix cradled his face. "Ethan, I love you. So much. I can't wait to have our own place, with a yard, somewhere for us to build a life. I was going to wait…

but what's the point. I love you. I know you might think I'm rushing things, but will you marry me?"

Ethan blinked at Felix, seeing a mix of hope and fear in his boyfriend's expression, then stared at him, his chest tight. "No! You can't ask me that!"

"What?" Felix's eyes widened. "You don't have to say yes, I didn't mean—"

"I have a ring for you," Ethan blurted. "Yes! Yes, I'll marry you, but only if you'll marry me right back."

Felix went from devastated to smiling in an instant. "That's kind of how it works, babe," Felix teased, and they kissed to seal the agreement, exchanging words of love, and commitment, and promising a future together.

A knock on the door separated them, and Felix sighed. "I guess we shouldn't mention the whole marriage thing now, I mean there are so many people we should be telling first."

"But what if the happy just bursts out of me?" Ethan asked, bemused, but Felix didn't get a chance to answer, because whoever was outside the door, the first of their guests, knocked again. Ethan was the one to open the door, Jared, Marcus and Neil, Rowan, and Caleb all clustered in the tiny landing waiting to be let in.

Ethan grasped Felix's hand and held tight, and they glanced at each other, and Ethan knew he couldn't keep his happy inside.

"We have news."

"They're getting married," Jared muttered to Caleb. "You owe me ten."

"You said they'd get engaged on Christmas Day, not

Eve," Caleb said, but he was grinning as he rooted in his pockets for a bill and slapped it into Jared's hand.

"Semantics," Jared said as he pulled Ethan into a hug. "Congratulations! Did you give him the ring yet?"

"Not yet," Ethan said, and Caleb frowned.

"Hang on," Caleb said. "You *knew* Ethan had a ring? I want my money back!" Bickering and laughing, with added congratulatory hugs, everyone moved inside, and Ethan closed the front door.

Then, he sat on his fiancé's lap, drank fizzy wine, ate cold pizza, and realized something very important.

With open doors, or closed ones, his life right now was pretty damn perfect.

THE END

Sapphire Cay

1. Follow the Sun
2. Under the Sun
3. Chase The Sun
4. Christmas In The Sun
5. Capture The Sun
6. Forever In The Sun

Also from RJ & Meredith

Standalone Christmas

- The Road to Frosty Hollow

Free Reads

- Stronger Together

Meet RJ Scott

RJ discovered romance in books at a very young age and realized that if there wasn't romance on the page, she could create it in her head. With over one hundred and fifty books published, she is a full time author of gay romance.

She lives and works out of her home in the beautiful English countryside, spends her spare time reading, watching films, and enjoying time with her family.

The last time she had a week's break from writing she didn't like it one little bit and has yet to meet a box of chocolates she couldn't defeat.

www.rjscott.co.uk | rj@rjscott.co.uk

NEWSLETTER - rjscott.co.uk/rjnews

f facebook.com/author.rjscott

instagram.com/rjscott_author

amazon.com/author/rj-scott

BB bookbub.com/authors/rj-scott

g goodreads.com/rjscott

patreon.com/RJScott

Meet Meredith Russell

Meredith Russell lives in the heart of England. An avid fan of many story genres, she enjoys nothing less than a happy ending. She believes in heroes and romance and strives to reflect this in her writing. Sharing her imagination and passion for stories and characters is a dream Meredith is excited to turn into reality.

www.meredithrussell.co.uk
meredithrussell666@gmail.com

facebook.com/meredithrussellauthor
x.com/MeredithRAuthor
instagram.com/miss_meredith_r